Disney·PIXAR

ELEMENTAL

Unlikely Friends

Design by Winnie Ho
Composition and layout by Susan Gerber

Published by Disney Press, an imprint of Buena Vista Books, Inc.
No part of this book may be reproduced or transmitted in any form
or by any means, electronic or mechanical, including photocopying,
recording, or by any information storage and retrieval system,
without written permission from the publisher. For information address
Disney Press, 1200 Grand Central Avenue, Glendale, California 91201.

Printed in the United States of America
First Hardcover Edition, May 2023
10 9 8 7 6 5 4 3 2 1
FAC-004510-23076

Library of Congress Control Number: 2022948649
ISBN 978-1-368-09245-6

Visit disneybooks.com

DISNEY · PIXAR

ELEMENTAL
Unlikely Friends

By Meredith Rusu

DISNEY PRESS

Los Angeles · New York

Prologue

Greetings, Bùrdì,

　I hope this letter finds its way to you. I have already departed Element City and am en route to the Kol Islands. Our ship left before the dawn's first rays. But the stories are true, my friend! Element City—it is <u>wondrous</u>! I never dreamed such a place could exist. Buildings so tall you could touch the sun. Lights burning like stars at all hours of the night. There are Elements from all over the world there—even Fire people! I saw them! One could easily become engulfed. I stayed only two sunrises, yet I could have explored my whole life and not seen everything.

　You are right to feel the spark of inspiration ignited by such a city. Bùrdì, in a place like this, you and your wife could open a shop and have customers flowing like lava. Your child would have opportunities unlike any in Fire Land—potential that would never be snuffed out.

I am only sorry I cannot be there to greet you. My brother awaits me in the Kol Islands, and I do not know when my travels will take me back. But I hope that, one day, we will burn side by side again.

Safe travels, Bùrdì. May the Blue Flame guide your path.

Chapter 1

Bùrdì and his wife, Síddèr, traveled in a small boat headed for unfamiliar territory. The ornamental lantern holding the Blue Flame of their beloved Fire Land glowed steadily, burning with a soft radiance that enveloped them both like a comforting blanket. With just their Blue Flame lantern and two suitcases, the couple had brought only the essentials to this new land. But the most precious thing of all had yet to arrive.

Bùrdì rested his cheek on Síddèr's pregnant belly. "Our new home, my child," he said in his native Firish language.

The baby responded with a swift kick to Bùrdì's head. A deep welling of hope and love bubbled up within Bùrdì and Síddèr, and for the briefest of moments, the Fire couple had the world to themselves. Bùrdì couldn't believe this was truly happening.

The journey they had dreamed about for so long was becoming a reality.

Overhead, a hot-air balloon drifted by and disappeared into the mist that rose above the approaching city. There it was! There was no mistaking the monumental skyscrapers with their spinning wind turbines or the high-speed water highways where vehicles whooshed by so fast their wakes made tidal waves. This magnificent place where few Fire people had ever dared to venture but where Bùrdì was determined to start their new life.

This was Element City.

The boat docked with a thud. Half-dazed, the Fire couple collected their bags and disembarked. Despite the whirlwind of commotion on the docks, an invisible bubble surrounded Bùrdì and Síddèr. Two Fire people arriving in Element City—a metropolis designed by Water and Earth and Air people, *for* Water and Earth and Air people—was an unusual sight indeed.

Nevertheless, excitement gleamed bright in Bùrdì's deep eyes as he ushered Síddèr into the Immigration Hall and up to the counter, where an Earth official, a tree stump growing atop his head, stood guard.

"Name?" the immigration official said without looking up.

"Útrí dàr ì Bùrdì," said Bùrdì.

"Fâsh ì Síddèr," added his wife.

Now the immigration official did look up. A confused expression cracked the bark lines around his face. "How do we spell that?" he asked hesitantly.

Bùrdì spelled his and Sìddèr's names, but to the official, it sounded like crackling fire.

The official had an idea. "You know what? Let's just go with Bernie and Cinder."

With an authoritative thunk, the official stamped his wooden nose onto an ink pad and then again onto an immigration document.

Bùrdì took the paper in his hands carefully, so as not to singe the edges, and read the names: "Bernie" and "Cinder." He liked them! Those were the names they would go by now—the names of two Elements that *belonged* in this great city. They were officially a part of this new world.

"Welcome to Element City!" the official announced.

Hand in hand, Bernie and Cinder stepped through the giant doors of the hall and into the streets.

Element City was *nothing* like Fire Land.

Everything here was so shiny and sparkling and new. Skyscrapers made entirely of glass stretched up toward the heavens, glinting in the sun. Visible through the windows were twisting spiral staircases made from vines dotted with pink and red and orange and yellow flowers: an actual rainbow of stairs ascending fifty stories high. Where Bernie and Cinder's homeland had bubbling volcanoes smoldering in the distance, Element City boasted an endless horizon of elegant and airy apartments. In Fire Land, the air had always been thick with the smoky scent of kol nuts and lava bread. But in Element City, everything smelled . . . *wet*. Canals crisscrossed every street with people traveling by boats.

The people. Bernie and Cinder had never seen *so many people*. Never-ending throngs of Earth, Water, and Air Elements bustling in a symphony of just barely controlled chaos.

The Fire couple stared in amazement. It was incredible. And overwhelming.

Without realizing it, Bernie walked straight through an Air person carrying a briefcase.

"Hey, watch it, Sparky!" the Air person shouted angrily.

Bernie gave the person an apologetic look. He had never walked *through* a person before. Thank goodness no one had gotten hurt! But still, it felt . . . weird.

A sudden cascade of water splashed down from a nearby elevated train track, startling Cinder and causing her to jump back, protecting her belly. But Bernie took his wife's hand, and cradling their Blue Flame lantern, he led the way up a steep staircase to a train platform high above.

While they waited patiently for the next train to arrive, Bernie studied a pictorial map of the city and pointed to a section outlined in green. "There!" he told Cinder in Firish. "The houses there have rooms for rent—that is what my friend told me. That is where we will start our new life."

Bernie had heard stories of Fire people who had left their homeland to seek out fresh opportunities in the distant Element City. Though details of success or failure were scarce, the hope those stories had given him had been like kindling just waiting for a spark. *Customers as far as the eye can see*, the tales had gone. *A city protected from harm. A haven for all Elements!* All they needed to find was a small apartment. Nothing too elaborate. Just something warm and cozy and safe. Then he would build his shop.

And *then* they could start their life together, the way he had promised Cinder.

The way they hadn't been able to in Fire Land.

Without warning, the train car they had boarded lurched, and a Water person stumbled right into Cinder. A big globule of his water splashed onto her, putting out half her head! Cinder whimpered, and Bernie quickly gave her some firewood from his satchel to bolster her flame back to normal. Once he was sure she was okay, Bernie shot the Water person a glare.

"What?" The Water person shrugged, unperturbed by the close call.

"Hmmmm," Bernie grumbled to himself. "Water."

Yet all thoughts of the incident were snuffed from his mind as he and Cinder stepped off the train car at the Green Village stop. The stone buildings here were simply *exquisite*. Rust-brown townhomes lined the streets, each engraved with elaborate carvings of plants and flowers. Cinder breathed in and held her belly lovingly. What a beautiful place to raise their baby!

Bernie bounded up the front steps of a townhome with a FOR RENT sign taped to the window and knocked on the door.

Footsteps thudded from within, and a weathered, old-growth Earth landlord with gnarled vine glasses answered.

Cinder greeted him in Firish. She and Bernie smiled wide to show that they were kind and trustworthy.

But an ill-timed gust of wind swept past, catching one of the embers from Bernie's fire. The spark drifted toward the landlord and landed directly on the crunchy, browning mop of leaves on his head. With a flash, the leaves burned to a crisp! The landlord's eyes grew wide with alarm. He stared at the two strangers—whose entire bodies were made of fire—and quickly slammed the door in their faces.

Bernie blinked. The landlord hadn't even given him a chance to show that they had enough money saved to afford the apartment. Still, dry leaves and fire probably weren't a good mix.

With a shrug, Bernie led Cinder to the next available home to rent.

But every building they visited had the same result.

Bernie knocked on the window of a smaller, more simply sculpted stone home in Green Village.

"Not available!"

Cinder pressed the doorbell of an apartment on Stratus Street, accidentally setting it on fire.

"Puff off!"

They greeted a Water landlord outside the streamlined condos of Waterson Way. He immediately started to boil!

"No steamers allowed!"

Tired and disheartened, Bernie led his weary wife to a desolate section of town far from the thrum of activity and fragrance of flowers. Their adventure was getting off to a rockier start than he had anticipated. He could see the light of optimism fading from Cinder's eyes. But they had made it this far. They couldn't give up now!

That was when he saw it. Another sign, peeling and chipped, but like a beacon of hope: a crimson FOR SALE notice posted outside a crumbling brick building in the most run-down part of Element City.

A *store* building.

Bernie practically leapt across the canal running just outside the building and rushed inside. It was perfect!

True, the abandoned store was dilapidated. The windows needed replacing. But with a little sand, he could make some new glass. That was a Fire specialty! Sure, he could see the glowing sunset peeking in through holes in the brick wall, and those leaking pipes along the roof would need to go. But *this* was something he could work with. A store he could build with his own two hands. An opportunity to create what couldn't be created back home. Finally, a chance for success!

Cinder raised a skeptical eyebrow as she dodged the water from a leaky pipe. But seeing her husband's excitement strengthened her own courage. How could she say no when she could see Bernie's dream literally shining in his eyes?

And so, soon afterward, with makeshift metal patches covering holes in the ceiling to protect them from the downpour of rain, Bernie and Cinder welcomed the cries of a brand-new Fire baby within the brick walls of their building.

"*Íkì ss ûr,*" whispered Cinder, cradling the glowing infant. *It's a girl.*

Bernie felt he would burst from the depth of love that burned in his heart. "*Bê ss ksòrif.*" *She's so perfect.*

Very carefully, he reached inside their lantern and cupped a bit of Blue Flame into his hands, then tenderly poured it over the tiny baby's head.

The baby's eyes widened as she felt the warmth of the Blue Flame flow over her. She cooed. Then sneezed.

Bernie laughed and took the cuddly bundle into his arms, touching his forehead to hers.

"Welcome, my Ember," he whispered, "to your new life."

Chapter 2

"Is it time yet, Àshfá? Is it time? Is it time? Is it time?"

Four-year-old Ember Lumen leapt around the store, leaving little scorch marks wherever her bare feet touched the freshly laid tiles.

"We just finished the floors. I do not remember fire footprints being part of the design," Bernie chided his very excited daughter, though he couldn't help smiling at her enthusiasm.

"But I'm ready to go!" Carefree, Ember hopped up on the ledge of her family's Blue Flame cauldron and swung her glowing legs, casting reflections on all the bright and shiny surfaces in the store. If a customer hadn't known any better, they would have thought the store had always looked this well maintained. Gone were the crumbling walls and boarded windows. In their place were thick glass windows that gleamed along the storefront and freshly mortared brick that rose to meet hand-forged iron beams supporting the ceiling. Pipes that had once carried water were now painted black as a testament to their purely ornamental nature.

Though the shop wasn't complete yet, it was getting there. Tools were being packed away, and shipping crates all the way from Fire Land had started to arrive, the authentic wares inside waiting patiently to be stacked on display shelves. Little by little, everything was coming together. Bernie had even decided on a name for the family's new shop: the Fireplace. His dream come true, a tribute to his homeland embodied in the store he'd built with his own two hands.

"You said we could see the Vivisteria flower at ten o'clock. It's ten o'clock!" Ember pointed insistently to a sun-shaped clock on the wall. The timepiece did not, in fact, read ten o'clock. Four-year-old Ember could not tell time yet, and it was barely a quarter to nine in the morning. But four-year-old Ember also liked to insist that many things were the way she wanted them to be.

"Be patient, my little fire flower. You must be steady, like the Blue Flame." Bernie guided his daughter's attention to the cauldron where their sacred Blue Flame shone, filling the shop with reverent energy. "Watch how it burns strong, but not wild. It is constant, always there when we need it. Our Blue Flame holds all our traditions and gives us strength to burn bright."

Ember's round eyes reflected the flame's glow as she stared deep into the cauldron. This was one of her favorite places to sit in the whole shop. Sometimes, while her parents had been hard at work sawing and nailing and hammering, Ember had curled up at the base of the cauldron with her favorite toy (a pretty Fire doll stitched from the softest fireproof silk), and she'd fallen asleep with the Blue Flame's warmth covering her like a snuggly blanket.

"The Blue Flame is all the way from Fire Land?" Ember asked her àshfá for the hundredth time.

"Yes, all the way from Fire Land." Bernie nodded. "We must always protect it. As long as we have the Blue Flame, we will remember who we are and where we came from."

"Can I go to Fire Land?" Ember asked curiously.

Bernie tapped her nose. "Perhaps, one day. But today we're going to see the Vivisteria flower."

"Oh yeah!" Ember leapt up, all thoughts of Fire Land popping out of her head. "Can we go now? Please, Àshfá?"

Bernie chuckled. "I'll drink one cup of lava java, then we'll go."

The line leading to see the Vivisteria flower was impossibly long. Ember leaned out so far that she nearly slipped out of her àshfá's grasp. She had never seen so many people in her life! Only once before had she left home with her parents, and she hadn't seen much on that trip, because her mother had clutched her so tightly to her chest on the train ride that Ember had felt like a little kol nut ready to pop. She had a vague memory of big buildings looming overhead as her parents ran through the streets, all the while repeating the words "clouds" and "rain" and "permits due." But Ember had been very little then. Now she was a big girl—four, nearly five!—and today was the biggest day of her life.

She couldn't believe how *busy* Element City was. Everywhere she looked there was a sea of activity. Hot-air balloons whizzed overhead, carrying waving families with Air children hanging precariously over the basket edges. Water trains splashed past on a never-ending schedule, opening their doors to release streams of passengers. There were tall tree Earth people on the sidewalks and short stump sproutlings running in the grass and screeching cars and dinging bikes and . . . So. Much. Noise!

"Àshfá, how are we going to get through?" Ember asked.

"Fire always finds a way," Bernie reassured her. "Look. Do you see those tall glass buildings? Those are the first buildings your mother and I saw when we arrived in Element City!"

Ember squinted toward where her father was pointing. Towering skyscrapers made entirely of glass twinkled in the morning sunlight, reflecting the blue of the coastal waters beyond.

"Wow!" she breathed. One hundred of her àshfá's shops could fit inside those. If she climbed to the top, she could probably touch the sun! "Is that where we have to go?" Ember asked in wonder.

"No, no." Bernie shook his head. "We're going there—Garden Central Station."

Ember looked ahead, beyond the ebb and flow of people, and gasped. A beautiful circular building with floor-to-ceiling glass windows stretched an entire city block. Ornate leaves and vines twisted along its wavy white rooftop like a living tapestry of art. And plastered everywhere were banners promoting the rare Vivisteria flower—on display for a limited time only!—the one and only flower of its kind. Ember's parents had told her *all* about the Vivisteria flower. It was the only plant in the whole wide world that could exist in any climate—even fire—meaning it was the only flower in the whole wide world Ember could actually *touch*! She had dreamed of touching a real flower all her life! Well, at least ever since her parents had read her a story about it in *Dr. Dante's Nursery Rhymes for Little Sparks.*

Of all the flowers dear, just one can fire draw near.
The Vivisteria bloom, like summer sun in June,
will grow with beauty bright no matter a fire's might.

19

Ember was so excited; her chest was bubbling like lava. Luckily, despite the massive crowd, Bernie and Ember seemed to have a little pocket of space to themselves. Ember liked that. It meant she couldn't accidentally singe another Element. Her àshfá had reminded her over and over again before their trip into the big city that she had to stay close to him and *not touch anyone*. But her àshfá had been silly to worry. No one ever seemed to come close to them. They'd even had a section of seats all to themselves on the train ride over. And the train had been packed! Maybe everyone realized how excited she was to see the Vivisteria flower, and they didn't want her to feel crowded.

"Are we almost to the front?" she asked, bouncing on her father's shoulders.

"Almost," her àshfá promised. "Be patient. The Vivisteria isn't going anywhere."

Ember noticed an Earth family standing near them and waved. "It's almost our turn!" she called. But they must not have heard her, because they turned away. Ember twisted to look behind the back of her father's brightly burning head and noticed a little Water boy about her age playing with some dewdrops on a staircase banister. She giggled as he scooped the water up into his hand.

"I'm going to touch the Vivisteria flower!" she announced. "My àshfá said I could! Are you going to touch it?"

The boy looked up, and his eyes grew super wide. Before he could answer, his mother whirlpooled him protectively to the center of their group.

Maybe he's too little to touch the flower, Ember thought. *But I'm not too little. I'm not afraid to touch the flower.* She puffed out her chest. *And everyone is going to see me!*

Chapter 3

"Ahhhhh! A *sponge*! Get it away!"

Five-year-old Wade Ripple streaked along the beachfront, running for dear life in the opposite direction of a particularly harmless-looking green sea sponge. His water legs sloshed as he sprinted, forming splatter footprints in the sand like water balloon bursts.

"Wade!" his father, Dewey, yelled. "Slow down! It's just a sponge! It's not going to hurt you!"

"Yes, it *will*!" Wade cowered behind a rock. "Is it gone? Did you take it away?"

Wade squeezed his eyes shut and couldn't stop sniffling as his father's footsteps approached.

When he opened his eyes, there was his dad—holding the sponge.

"AHHHHHHHH!" screamed Wade.

"Son, relax!" Dewey desperately tried to reassure him. "It's already soaked, see? It can't absorb any more water."

"But what if there's a little bit of space left?" Wade blubbered. "It will suck me in!"

"Son, nobody has ever gotten stuck inside a sea sponge forever."

"*I* did!" Wade insisted. "At school! The other day! It was just lying there on the floor. Mr. Pine forgot to put it in his cart. I tried to help him. And the sponge *sucked me in*!"

Wade's dad tried to stifle a chuckle. "It was just an accident. Ms. Drizzle told me she got you right out."

"No, I was in there *forever*." Wade sobbed. "Ms. Drizzle didn't find me until after recess."

"Really?" His father frowned. "That long? Hmmm. I'm going to have a talk with her."

Wade howled. "Now I can't even go back to school!"

"That's silly. Wade, come on. I need you to be strong." Dewey flexed his arms to demonstrate. "You're a big boy now. You're not a little puddle anymore."

But Wade sobbed and sobbed. With a heavy sigh, his father pulled the inconsolable Water child closer, feeling every ebb and flow of the young boy's chest.

"These feelings you've got, they're pretty big, huh?" he asked. "Like a tidal wave you can't stop?"

"Uh-huh." Wade wiped away a blubbery sniffle.

"You know what's bigger?" his father asked. And when Wade shook his head, Dewey pointed out at the ocean.

"The ocean?" asked Wade.

"The ocean." His dad nodded. "That's the biggest, widest water you're going to find in this whole wide world. Everything just flows out there. It keeps stretching and spreading thinner and thinner until it's just . . . calm."

Wade sniffled again. "You want me to go into the ocean?"

"No, no." His father laughed and hugged him tight. "I don't want you to go into the ocean. I want you to put your *feelings* into the ocean. Your big feelings. The ones that are so big and make you so scared it's like you can't control them."

Wade stared out at the shimmering water. It stretched so far he couldn't see the end.

"But how?" he asked. "How do I put my feelings in the ocean?"

"Let me show you."

Dewey stood up and walked to the edge of the foaming sea. Then, with an unexpected burst, he screamed.

"AHHHHHHHHHHHHHHHHH!"

His voice echoed, hanging over the water before getting swept up in the sound of the sea and the wind and the crashing waves. Then he turned with a big grin toward his son.

"See?" He spread his arms wide. "That water's so big it can handle anything, even the biggest feelings. My papa used to tell me, 'There's no emotion without the ocean.' You try it. Scream your big feelings into the ocean. Let the water spread them out and smooth them away until you just feel . . . calm."

Wade hesitantly got to his feet, wiped his eyes, and walked up beside his dad.

"Ahh," he bleated. "Like that?"

"Louder," his father said encouragingly.

"Ahhhh!" Wade tried again.

"Better," his father said. "But come on. Really let that ocean have it! That sponge trapped you inside it! Show me what it felt like. Send it out to sea!"

Wade sucked in a breath so deep it filled his entire chest with one ginormous air bubble, and then . . .

"AHHHHHHHHHHHHHHHH!!!!!"

He screamed with all the might his bubbly little chest could muster. He screamed until he couldn't tell where his voice ended and where the crashing ocean waves began.

When he finally stopped, his chest felt empty. His throat felt uncomfortably dry. But he also felt . . . lighter? Like he had let go of something heavy he hadn't even realized he had been holding on to.

"That's my boy." Wade's father splashed the top of the little boy's head. "I told you, there isn't anything the ocean can't take."

Chapter 4

"I can't take it!"

Bernie's angry voice echoed up through the vents from the main part of the store. Ember lay quietly in her bed, turning her doll over in her hands.

"Hush!" her mother warned. "Ember will hear you."

But Bernie continued, undaunted. "How dare they turn away a little kid!"

There was a pause and some more murmuring that Ember couldn't hear. She leaned closer to the vent.

"The city rules were not made with Fire in mind." Ember could just make out her mother's words.

Another long pause.

"But she was so excited," her àshfá finally said. His voice

sounded strange—kind of crackly. "You should have seen her face. She asked me what she did wrong. Why they did not let her in."

"She is little," her mother said. "She will forget."

"*I* will not forget." Bernie's voice hardened, the way it did when a city inspector showed up late or an unexpected rain shower sent them running for cover. "If we are not welcome there, *they* are not welcome here."

There was a scuffling of chairs scraping against the floors as the kettle whistled and her mother hurried to turn it off.

Ember rolled over in her bed, putting her doll against her lips. Just a few hours before, she and her àshfá had reached the entrance to Garden Central Station. A guard stuck out his arm in front of them, blocking their path. He said they couldn't go in—they weren't allowed. But everyone else was allowed. Even the little Water boy who was younger than Ember. Only she and her àshfá were turned away.

Ember had never seen her àshfá so angry before. He yelled and stamped his foot and sent licks of fire flying around them that made people back away. Ember still didn't know what they had done wrong. They hadn't cut in line. They'd waited just like everyone else. But the guard wouldn't let them pass, and all the people had been staring at them.

Downstairs, her parents' voices were too low now for her to hear.

Ember closed her eyes. Her àshfá had promised they would see the Vivisteria flower another time. She had wanted to ask when, but her àshfá's flames were still flaring angrily on the train ride home, so she hadn't dared. Maybe she would ask tomorrow. He had promised it wasn't their fault. That they had done nothing wrong.

So it wasn't their fault . . . right?

Tiny tears smoldered on her cheeks before they even reached her pillow. She thought of the words the guard had shouted at them before they left.

"Go back to Fire Land!"

She didn't understand. They didn't *live* in Fire Land. Element City was their home.

What had he meant?

"I want to help!"

Ember ran right underneath the large sign her parents were hauling toward the front of the store and pressed her hands to the bottom, attempting to help hold it up. It had been five months since the Vivisteria incident, and in that time, two big things had happened: Ember had turned five (she was officially a big kid!) and, at long last, the fateful day had arrived.

Tomorrow was the Fireplace's grand opening.

"Ember, be careful!" her mother cautioned. "You could get crushed and snuffed out."

"No, I won't," Ember said confidently. "I'm five now. I'm strong!"

"Hah! Good daughter!" Bernie said proudly. "Strong like her àshfá!"

"Exactly like her àshfá," Cinder quipped. "Strong *and* stubborn."

Bernie and Cinder carefully placed the sign down on the ground without crushing or snuffing out their daughter, and Ember skipped around in front of the sign to read the words her àshfá had emblazoned across the front.

"The Fireplace!" she read proudly to her mom. "Look, Àshká! I did that! I did that!"

Ember pointed to a little fire symbol scorched at the top of the sign. The markings weren't as steady as her father's fire calligraphy. But it was pretty good, if Ember said so herself.

"It's true." Her father patted the top of Ember's fiery head. "And now it will welcome customers to our shop every day, just like a traditional Fire Land store."

Ember watched curiously as her àshfá climbed the ladder. "What's it like in Fire Land?"

"Hot," Bernie grunted, maneuvering the sign's hook onto a wrought-iron bar above the front door.

"Is that why you left?" Ember asked. "Because it's too hot?"

Bernie chuckled. "Not hotter than me. Our family burns bright!"

Bernie held his breath and blew up a giant flame on top of his head—one of Ember's favorite tricks! She clapped.

"There." Bernie climbed down and surveyed his handiwork. "We are ready for opening day. What do you think?"

Ember gazed through the glass front door of her parents' shop. The display shelves were packed with food and trinkets straight from Fire Land. Twinkling glass bead necklaces. Squiggly lollipops twisted from scratch. And so many snacks! She thought it was the most beautiful thing she had ever seen in her entire life.

The crisp air steamed at her nostrils. Even outside, the spicy scent of kol nuts wafted from inside the store. Tomorrow was the big day. Her parents had been posting announcement flyers around their section of town for weeks. Would there be a line of people waiting when Ember woke up? she wondered. Would they sell out of everything? Would they be *on the news*?

"This shop will be the pride of our family," Bernie asserted. "And someday, Ember, it will all be yours."

"Mine?" Ember gasped. "The shop will be mine?"

"One day." He gave her shoulder a squeeze. "When you are big like me!" He flexed his arms and flared up his fire again. Ember jumped up and down excitedly while Cinder shook her head, though she, too, was smiling.

"This is *our* Fireplace!" Bernie announced loudly enough for the whole block to hear, though no one was around. "No one will water us down!"

"Oh, Bernie." Cinder sighed. "Come. We must wrap the kol nuts, then go to bed. We need rest for the grand opening."

As Ember's parents headed inside, she lingered behind, staying for just a moment longer to gaze at the glowing storefront. She couldn't believe it. One day, this would be *her* shop!

She couldn't think of anything she had ever wanted more in her life.

Chapter 5

"Two kol nuts, please!"

"Is the toast-roast lava java still on sale?"

"Mama, can I have a lollipop?"

"No—you already had two. Your tummy will crystallize."

"But I *want* another lollipop!"

The Fireplace was bursting with activity as customers weaved in and out of the shelves, curiously examining all the authentic Fire Land wares. Teenaged Ember stood behind the counter, taking it all in. And she smiled.

The Fireplace had come a long way in a few years.

So had the whole Fire community.

Word had spread once Bernie and Cinder opened the Fireplace. "A corner of Element City built *for* Fire?" people had asked. "No fear of being watered down?" Unlike the rest of Element City, where the canals lining the streets frequently filled with water spillover, the canals here remained dry so that Fire could flourish. That particular achievement had been Bernie's pride and joy: receiving approval from the city to officially close the canal doors leading into this section of town. Back then, the officials had considered this section of the city too dilapidated for anyone to care if canal access would be restricted. Little did they know, Bernie had been determined to make this corner of town a haven for all Fire people. *Very* determined.

Once the canals had closed, little by little, more Fire people had arrived. Some from other areas of town that were less . . . welcoming. Others on ships sailing directly from Fire Land. Signs had been written in native Firish. Traditional Fire Land holidays were celebrated. There was even a massive bonfire held once a year on All Ash's Eve that drew spectators from far and wide.

All of it started because of one little shop that would someday be Ember's.

"Ember!" her mother called from behind a beaded curtain, where she was performing a smoke reading for a young Fire couple. "Please watch the hot logs so they don't burn."

"On it!" Ember spun and turned off the heat from the burners in one swift movement. She transferred the freshly cooked hot logs to the warming rollers without spilling a single drop of spicy oil.

"Excuse me?" An exhausted mother walked up to the counter with her Fire child, who was crying streams of burning tears. "I'm afraid we need one more lollipop. Is there any way you could make another one?" The beleaguered mother looked down at her weeping son, clearly too tired to argue with him anymore. But Ember grinned.

"One lollipop, coming up!" Ember collected a scoop of sugar in her hands and, with masterful flourish, melted the crystals into a sticky, shimmering strand. Always excited to test out her sculpting skills, she molded it into a simplified version of the boy's face.

"Wow." The little boy stopped crying and took the lollipop. He stared at it for a long moment before shoving the treat into his mouth all at once.

The grateful mother paid just as Ember's àshfá walked up to the counter. "Your daughter is quite the artist," she said.

"She is a good daughter." Bernie nodded approvingly. "And one day, this will all be hers."

"Today?" Ember asked, raising her eyebrows in mock hope.

Bernie laughed. "When you are ready."

A short while later, after the lunchtime rush had settled down and the aisles were quiet, Ember carefully arranged glass trinkets on the front shelves. She liked how the perfectly cut edges of each sculpture captured the light in just the right way. Sometimes, when no one was looking, she would use a bit of sand to add an extra glass curlicue or ripple to the pieces, making them true Fireplace originals.

She picked up a pretty glass Vivisteria flower, tilting it so it glistened in the afternoon light. This was the closest she would ever get to touching a Vivisteria, she figured. The big feelings from that day long before had dulled, but the echoes remained. The world had seemed different back then. Element City had seemed different back then. She had a vague memory of wishing she could climb to the top of the glass towers by the ocean's edge as a young girl, hoping to reach the sun. But now, Ember's ambitions were much more firmly planted. Here, in the Fire section of town, it was her responsibility to carry on the old Fire traditions just like her àshfá had taught her. Right here in her àshfá's shop, she would always feel at home.

"Ember, please come help me with the kol nuts," Bernie called.

Brushing her thoughts aside, Ember headed dutifully behind the counter, strapping on an ash-stained apron.

"Àshfá?" she asked as she grabbed a log and squeezed it between her hands to create the bite-sized pieces of kol nuts. "What's it like in Fire Land?"

"Humph," Bernie grunted, chopping at a much slower pace. "Hot."

"You always say that. But what's it like, living with only Fire people?"

"Less wet," Bernie said shortly. "No troublemaking Water teenagers to keep an eye on."

"Hah!" Ember thought back to the time two mischievous Water teens had tried splashing out a whole aisle of flame souvenirs when she was younger. Despite being half their age, she'd had the boldness to sneak up behind them and flare so big that their splashy punk hairstyles had started to boil. "You splash it, you buy it!" she'd shouted as they scampered out of the store. Her àshfá had been so proud.

"But didn't you know there would be more Water people here when you came?" she asked.

Bernie considered this. "We made a home for Fire people here. Together, we burn bright."

Ember paused. "Then why did you leave Fire Land in the first place?"

Bernie shook his head. "Too many questions. Clearly you don't have enough work to keep busy!"

"Oh, I have plenty of work," Ember bantered back, making kol nuts even faster. "But seriously. We have a whole shop dedicated to Fire Land, and we keep all the old Fire Land traditions, but you and Àshká barely ever talk about what it was like growing up there. I've never even seen pictures. *Why* did you guys leave?"

"Mmmm." Bernie pushed his completed kol nuts to the side. "Hand me another log."

"There isn't another one." Ember brushed her hands on her apron. "They're all done."

Bernie looked up in surprise to see that the kol nuts were all finished, and Ember's pile was triple the size of his.

"Ah!" he said, genuinely impressed. "Good daughter!"

Just then, the bell by the front register dinged. A Fire customer with thick glasses and a metal basket full of trinkets was waiting to check out.

"How about . . ." Bernie said slowly, "you take it today?"

Ember sucked in her breath. "For real?" she asked, her heart beating fast. Her àshfá *never* asked her to help with checkout. Working the register was strictly for him and her mother. This was a big deal! Her chance to prove she had what it took to run the store someday!

Removing her apron, she walked confidently over to the register, barely able to contain the giddy grin spread across her face.

"*Rái khíf!*" she greeted the customer, who was squinting at the promotional signs posted by the register. "How can I help you?"

"All this." The customer pushed the basket toward her without looking up. "And . . . the sparklers are buy one, get one free?"

"That's right!" Ember said cheerfully, beginning to ring up his items.

"Great!" The customer grabbed a sparkler and set it alight. "I'll take the free one."

Ember stopped ringing. *Huh? What is this guy talking about?*

"Oh, no, you see, you need to *buy* one to get one free," she explained helpfully. Just to be safe, she took the sparkler from his hand and gently blew it out so it wouldn't burn to the end before he'd purchased one for real.

Now the customer's squinty eyes turned toward Ember. "But I just want the free one," he insisted, taking another sparkler and lighting it up.

Ember felt an odd tightness in her chest. Was this guy just messing with her?

"Sorry, that's not how this works," she said, still trying to be helpful but a bit more forcefully. Again, she blew the sparkler out.

The man took another one. "But the customer is always right."

Ember smiled, gritting her teeth. "Not in this case."

The customer snatched sparklers one by one from the bucket, setting each on fire. And Ember grabbed them back one by one and snuffed them out, until she was holding an entire bouquet of half-burned sparklers.

What was this guy thinking? He was going to ruin the whole batch! Of all the times to have a difficult customer, it had to be on her very first time manning the checkout. What was his problem?

"Just give me one for free!" the man shouted at Ember, little flecks of fire spittle hitting her cheek.

Ember felt her flame flaring. "THAT'S. NOT. HOW. THIS. WORKS!"

Before Ember even realized what she was doing, her fire blazed so hot she burst in an explosion of anger, setting everything around her on fire!

KABOOM!

When the smoke cleared, Ember found herself breathing heavily, staring in shock at the ash-riddled countertop. The basket of souvenirs had completely melted, and the customer still stood before her, blinking in surprise behind his heat-twisted glasses.

"Oh!" Bernie ran up to take charge, grabbing a few spare sparklers from an unscorched display and shoving them into the blob of melted items. "Happy birthday!" he exclaimed. Then he gently ushered a still smoldering Ember out from behind the register.

"What just happened?" he asked, concerned. "Why did you lose your temper?"

"I—I don't know." Ember couldn't stop shaking. "He was pushing and pushing, and I just—"

"Calm, calm." Bernie patted her back. "Sometimes customers can be tough. Just take a breath and make a connection—*that's* the most important thing."

Ember nodded. She wanted to be calm for her àshfá. To prove it hadn't been her fault. But she was so worked up it was almost hard to breathe. Had she messed up her one shot? Would her àshfá think she couldn't handle the store now?

Bernie clearly saw how upset she was, because he took her hands. "Do not worry. I will help you. We will work on this together." He put her apron back on, smoothed out a wrinkle, and winked. "When you can connect with the customers and not lose your temper, then you will be ready to take over the shop."

Chapter 6

"But I set up that tryout appointment myself!" Wade's father sent ripples running through his head as he rubbed it, pacing back and forth in frustration. "I scheduled it specifically to make up for last month's tryout that you missed. I just don't understand. *How* could you forget?"

Sixteen-year-old Wade sat spread out on the inflatable couch in their living room as an actual puddle. His eyes looked tearfully up at his dad.

"The—the music," he blubbered.

His father stopped pacing. "The *what?*"

"The music!" Wade re-formed just enough for his father to see his head. "I was on my way to the waveball field when I heard the marching band practicing 'Monsoon Mambo.' It's my favorite song!"

"I don't understand. You listened to the song for a whole half hour?"

"No . . ." Wade sniffled. "I helped conduct the band."

Wade's father blinked. "You missed your waveball tryout because you were *conducting* the marching band?" Though the words came out of his mouth, it almost looked like he was trying to make sense of a different language.

"I told you he wouldn't understand, Mom!" Wade howled, and splashed into a puddle again. His mother instantly flowed over to her son.

"Don't be too disappointed with him, Dewey," Brook said mistily. "My baby boy can't help it if he's got the soul of a musician."

"But he's *not* a baby, Brook!" Wade's dad insisted. "He's a sixteen-year-old young man whose father went to great lengths to convince Coach Tide to even *give* him a second tryout. He's not even *in* the marching band!"

"Because you wouldn't let me join!" Wade exclaimed.

"Because you jumped from one instrument to the next and never practiced!" his father spluttered. "First it was the piccolo. Then it was the flute. And the tuba. And where is that tuba, Wade? It's submerged in your room somewhere!"

"But . . . but . . . the mambo!" Wade wailed, and puddled up next to his mom, who rocked him back and forth.

"My poor little drip, drip, baby boy," she sang soothingly. "Drip, drip, drip goes the baby boy."

Dewey turned to Wade's older brother, Alan, who effortlessly sank water balloon after water balloon into a makeshift fishnet hoop hanging from the door.

"Am I completely out to sea on this one?" Dewey asked, hoping for backup.

"Don't worry, Dad." Alan tossed yet another water balloon through the hoop. "I'll help train Wade so he doesn't always go to puddles."

"What if he wants to play puddle ball?" Wade's younger sibling, Lake, quipped from the corner, where they were using black ink to paint their nails. "Won't he need the puddles?"

"No one needs puddles," Alan retorted.

Wade howled even louder, and Dewey plopped down onto an inflatable armchair.

"It's not the puddles that get me upset." Dewey sighed. "The truth is I'd be okay with *anything* as long as he just . . . picked! One day it's the mambo. The next day it's pottery. The day after that, it's deep-sea philosophy." He put his face in his hands. "I just don't *get* it. When I was his age, my head was filled with thoughts of trophies and sports. Not lagoon mambos."

" 'Monsoon Mambo'!" Wade bawled.

"Whatever!" Wade's dad finally lost his temper. "You could be performing the mambo on Broadship Way and I would be happy as long you stuck with something!" An oversized air bubble formed in Dewey's chest, and he suddenly looked like he couldn't catch his breath. He leaned against the armchair for a second, struggling to inhale deeply.

"You okay, Dad?" Alan stopped shooting hoops.

"Dewey?" Brook hurried over. "Should I call Dr. Coral? It's not good for you to get so bubbled up."

"No, no, I'm fine." Dewey took a few moments to compose himself before turning back to Wade. "Son, I am behind you in whatever you choose. I just want you to pick before you run out of options. There are only so many currents in the course of a man's life. If you don't figure out which one you want to follow, you'll wind up adrift."

With a startling surge, Wade stood to his full form. "I'm sorry I'm not *like* you, Dad! I might not have everything figured out. But it's not the end of the world if I just go with the flow!"

"Sounds like someone's having an identity crisis," Lake said snarkily.

"You all just don't understand!" Wade cried. Then, bursting into a full downpour of tears, he tore from the room and slammed the door to his bedroom, sending an angry wave pulsing through the living room pool.

Brook wept.

Alan sniffled.

A single angsty teardrop ran down Lake's cheek.

And Dewey sank deeper into the inflatable armchair.

When had raising kids become this hard?

Chapter 7

A small stone glistened at the edge of the construction site, and Wade Ripple, now a grown man wearing a hard hat and a construction worker safety vest, stopped to examine it. The pebble was so tiny, so round. And yet it fit perfectly in this concrete landscape.

"Do you ever wonder if we're all just tiny stones fitting into the large mosaic of life?" Wade mused.

An Earth worker next to him named Bark grunted, hauling a heavy bag of cement powder to the mixing machine.

"You know what I mean." Wade swirled the pebble around the inside of his hard hat as he spoke. "Your family tree is huge. Have you ever wondered what would happen if one single branch hadn't stretched out in the way it did? The whole family foliage would be different."

"Hah. Where'd you find this kid, Rocco?" Bark's leaves rustled as he chuckled.

Rocco, the craggy construction foreman, didn't look up from his clipboard. "Begged me to give him a chance. Insisted construction was his calling. Very . . . persuasive."

"That so, kid?" Bark dropped three more heavy bags of cement, shaking loose a few of his browning leaves with the thud. "Always knew you wanted to be a construction worker?" Then he pointed to the cement mixer. "Help me fill this, would ya? Two bags to start."

"Oh, well, I didn't always know," Wade confessed as he awkwardly put his hard hat back on and hurried over. He sloshed as he moved— he'd grown a little watery around the middle since his slim-stream teenage days. "Years ago, I used to want to be in music."

"Music?" a Water worker named Bub interjected. "What kinda music?"

"Oh, anything, really," Wade said as he used a special machine to open a bag of concrete powder and pour it into the mixer. "I played the water glasses in the second-grade talent show once, but I kept accidentally filling them up with tears every time I made a mistake, so Ms. Marina told me to try something sturdier. Did the piccolo for a while. Even tried my hand at composing. Never got the notes just right."

Wade used the machine to begin pouring a second bag of cement powder. "How about you, Bub? You look like a yacht rock aficionado to me."

"Mmm." Bub nodded. "Nothing gets me in the party mood like that bubbly beat."

"See, that's what I'm talking about!" Wade eagerly gestured. "The rhythm is something you *feel* inside you. It's not about precision. It's about emotion."

"So then what are you doing here?" Bark asked, climbing up into the cement mixer cabin to check the settings.

"Ah, well, that's a long story." Wade sighed and started loading a third bag. "See, my dad wanted me to follow the family legacy and play waveball, like him. We never saw eye to eye on stuff like that." He emptied the bag into the mixer and tossed it aside. "He always insisted I needed to be more focused. Pick a current and stick with it. But *I* didn't know what I wanted. I just needed time to explore all the options, you know? I thought eventually I'd convince him to see my side. But then he died. So I never got the chance."

Even craggy old Rocco looked up from his clipboard at that. "I'm sorry, kid."

Wade felt globules of tears beading up around his eyes. "You always think you have more time, you know?" He sniffed.

"How long since your pops passed?" Bark asked.

"Ten years," Wade said, "when I was sixteen. I mean, I probably should have listened to him. But what kid has their whole life figured out by sixteen?"

The workers all shook their heads. Everyone was captivated by Wade's story now.

"My dad thought I should have," Wade said, a touch bitterly, as he poured another bag. "After he was gone, the joy of music just kind of—left. It didn't seem right to do something he thought was a waste of time."

"I wanted to be an actor," a stout Water worker named Swampy chimed in. Everyone looked at him in surprise, and he nodded. "It's true! That was *my* calling! ACTING!" He shook his fist in the air for emphasis. "But my old man got on me about duty and responsibility and being grounded. Construction was the only way to go after that. When did you realize you wanted to work in construction?" he asked Wade.

"Oh, I still don't know exactly what I want to do." Wade loaded another cement powder bag. What number was he on? Eh, it was a big machine. Couldn't hurt to have a little extra. "I've tried lots of things. Telemarketing. Water-taxi driving. Even worked as a salesperson for a sea-salt shipping company once."

"So what happened?" Rocco asked.

"Not sure," Wade said mistily, emptying the final bag. "Everyone was always so nice everywhere I got hired, and they all seemed to like me until things just . . . didn't work out."

"All set down there?" Bark asked from the control seat of the cement mixer.

"Oh, yeah!" Wade tossed the last empty bag to the ground. "You're good to go! Here, I'll even give you some extra water to mix things up nice and cement-y! Let's do this!"

Later that night, Wade found himself where he always found himself when he got fired from a job. By the side of the ocean.

He hadn't *meant* to pour so much cement powder into the mixer. He'd just gotten carried away by the flow of conversation, distracted—as always—by the stories everyone had to share.

The cement explosion had been impressive. Very impressive. The burst had looked almost like a volcanic eruption, except gray and squelchy. Somehow, Wade had made it out unscathed. The other workers, however, had gotten rather . . . stuck. They would be okay. It would take a while to chip all the excess cement away, but no one was hurt. The worst damage was that the construction site work would be set back by a few months while they dug everything out.

As for Wade, he wouldn't be there to help them. Because Rocco had fired him on the spot. Just like he'd been fired for losing an entire shipment of sea salt as he blubbered away to the other sales reps. And like he'd been let go after he got the mayor of Element City lost while chatting en route to a campaign event. And like, it seemed to Wade, he'd let down everyone in his life.

"I wish you were here, Dad," Wade said quietly, allowing the ocean foam to froth up inside his feet. "I just never seem to know which way to go."

Wade took a deep breath and screamed at the top of his lungs into the ocean, a soulful wail that swept along the sea, spreading farther and wider than any cry the wave-worn sand dunes had ever heard before.

Chapter 8

"Take a breath. Make a connection. Take a breath. Make a connection."

Ember opened her eyes. The customer was still standing there impatiently in front of her, holding out an empty kol-nut bag.

"Well?" the customer asked sharply. "Are you going to give me my money back or not?"

Ember breathed in deeply. "I'm afraid we can't refund eaten merchandise," she said in the slowest, calmest, most under-control voice she could muster.

"But they tasted like ash!" The customer wagged the empty bag in her face. "You sold me yesterday's batch. I want my money back!"

Ember felt anger spreading through her like hot lava.

"Take a breath . . ." she thought desperately.

"I've got a lot of followers on Insta-flame, you know," the customer said in a warning tone. "I'll bet they'd all like to know that the kol nuts here—"

"MAKE A CONNECTION!" Unable to control herself, Ember exploded in a near purple fireball, smashing the glass from the front counter display case. The empty bag disintegrated in the customer's hand.

Near the front of the store, two regulars, named Flarry and Flarrietta, sat at a table sipping lava java. "She almost went full purple!" Flarrietta whispered. "I've never seen anyone go full purple!"

Ember sighed, hugely embarrassed. "Sorry, everyone," she said, fumbling to collect the broken glass from the floor.

Meanwhile, Bernie rushed out of a back room, immediately recognizing what had happened. "Oh, please forgive my daughter," he said to the shell-shocked customer. "She burns bright, but sometimes *too* bright. Heh heh." He blew out a small flower on the customer's hat that was still on fire. "Nice hat, by the way. Come, let me make you a fresh batch. On the house."

Whatever complaints the customer originally had went up in smoke with the explosion. She nodded, staring forward with a wide, unfocused gaze.

"Sorry, Àshfá," Ember said again, picking up the last shards of glass. She tossed them into her mouth and munched them until they melted into a smooth, malleable gloop. "I don't know why that one got away from me."

"Did you count to ten?" Bernie asked. "Deep breaths? Picture them as tiny matchsticks?"

"All of it," Ember admitted between crunches.

"It is okay. You are tense because of the Red Dot Sale tomorrow." Bernie tried to comfort his daughter. "It has us all at a broil."

"Mmmph." Ember spit out the glowing glass and began shaping it with her hands. "I guess."

The truth was Ember *hadn't* been worried about the Red Dot Sale. It had been the furthest thing from her mind—not even cracking the top ten.

The top ten things on Ember's mind were the last ten years, all reaching back to her very first time behind the sales counter, and how at least once a week since, sometimes as much as once a day, she'd lost her temper with a customer. The specifics of the incidents had varied, and the customer's complaints changed, but the result was always the same: every time the now twenty-five-year-old Ember Lumen encountered a difficult customer, she exploded in a fiery ball of frustration.

"It's just, some of these customers, they get me all . . . *grrrrr*."

Ember angrily smoothed out the glass panel, accidentally smooshing the edge.

"I know, I know." Bernie empathized as he made a fresh batch of kol nuts. "Just do what we talked about. You are *so* good at everything else."

With a deep breath, Ember heated and pressed out the smooshed section of glass, re-forming the entire piece into a pristinely smooth panel. She picked it up and admired it, pleased. Glasswork was at least one thing she was good at.

Through the glass, she could see her àshfá working behind the counter. The ten long years had changed him, too. He looked so worn and tired that a fresh pang of guilt singed Ember's chest. He shouldn't be the one putting himself out to work day in and day out without a sick day, let alone a vacation. It should be her. It should have been her for years now. When Ember was still a teenager, her àshfá used to talk about retiring and taking it easy. About how, on that bright and shining day, he would finally pass the store keys into his daughter's trustworthy hands, and maybe he and her mother would even travel for a season to Fire Land while they still had a spark in their step. Ember had thrived on that hope, longing for her chance to finally be in charge, because that would be the day she *knew* she'd earned her àshfá's pride.

But with every passing temper explosion, talk of retirement had slowly dissipated. Worse, it had become almost taboo. Retirement wasn't spoken of anymore—not by the Lumen family, anyway.

"I'll get it," she promised her àshfá as she replaced the glass. "I just want you to rest."

Behind the counter, Bernie began coughing uncontrollably. Ember rushed to his side, steadying him.

"You okay?" she asked, her flames flickering with worry.

"Yes." Bernie coughed. "Just tired."

From across the store, the two regulars had been observing the entire exchange.

"Bernie, that cough is terrible," said Flarry.

"Almost as terrible as your cooking," added Flarrietta.

Everyone in the shop chuckled, including Bernie and Ember.

"Ê . . . shútsh." Bernie rolled his eyes and waved away the joke. He and these two characters went way back, almost to the grand opening of the Fireplace. Firetown wasn't Firetown without some steam punks to liven things up.

"When are you going to put Ember out of her misery and retire, huh?" Flarrietta prodded. "Finally put her name on the sign out there?"

Ember glanced out of the corner of her eye at her àshfá.

Bernie coughed again and nodded. "She'll take over when she's ready."

Ember sighed. Not the answer she wanted to hear.

"Speaking of ready"—she turned her attention to Flarry and Flarrietta—"we are *more* than ready for you to actually *buy* something if you'd ever get up off your lazy ash."

"Oh, burn!" the two regulars said in unison, and everyone in the store laughed again. Ember grinned. If there was one thing she had grown skilled at other than shaping glass, it was deflecting disappointment with wisecracks.

"But she is *so* close," Bernie added, perhaps seeing through his daughter's ruse. "I mean, she'll probably never do deliveries as fast as me . . ."

"Oh, you don't think I can beat your record?" Ember bantered back. It was funny how joking about her unmet expectations was better than not acknowledging it at all. "Because I've been taking it easy on you so I don't hurt your feelings, Mr. Smokestack." She grabbed her scooter goggles and cranked a timer. "Game on."

Chapter 9

The air hung thick with the sweet smell of incense. Two knowing eyes glowed through the haze, peering at the hopeful couple sitting across the table. The answer to the question burning in their hearts would be revealed in this very room.

"Before I see if you are a match, I will splash this on your heart to bring love to the surface." Cinder flicked a small amount of oil onto the young Fire people. They oohed as their flames turned red. Then they each lit a stick and watched as the tendrils of smoke rose into the air.

"And I will read the smoke," Cinder finished mystically. She leaned in to examine the curling gray mist. She sniffed it. Then . . .

Whoosh! The curtain to the smoke-reading room flew open. Ember stood silhouetted in the doorway, clearly on a mission.

"Ember!" Cinder admonished. "I'm doing a reading!"

"Sorry, Àshká." Ember stuffed parcels from the shelves into her delivery basket. "Going for Dad's record."

Meanwhile, the young couple waited anxiously for Cinder's verdict.

"So . . . are we a match?" they asked hopefully.

Snapping back into mystical mode, Cinder paused for dramatic effect before proclaiming, "It's true love!"

The happy couple embraced just as Ember finished collecting her deliveries.

"Which is more than I ever smelled on this one," Cinder jabbed her thumb in Ember's direction. She sniffed her daughter's arm as she passed, pursing her lips in disappointment. "Yup! Nothing. Just a loveless sad future of sadness."

Ember rolled her eyes. She'd heard this melodramatic criticism many times before. "Oh, goodie. This ol' chestnut."

Ember darted just out of reach of further scrutiny and whipped the curtain closed, sending a puff of dust billowing around Cinder. The woman sighed. What good was being the Firetown matchmaker if she couldn't even match her own daughter? Sometimes Cinder wondered if that girl's head was filled with just as many dreams of being a shopkeeper as her husband's. Thank the Blue Flame, Cinder had met Bernie *before* he opened his shop. Otherwise, she wasn't sure he would have stopped working long enough to recognize true love even if it had hit him in the face.

Behind Cinder, the young Fire couple had started kissing. A lot.

Cinder spritzed them with a water bottle, instantly sizzling out their romance.

"Save it for the wedding!"

Outside, Ember strapped boxes onto her scooter just as an Earth kid named Clod popped up from a planter pot.

"Yo, yo, yo, Ember!" Clod shouted, his voice cracking.

"Yo, Clod," Ember said offhandedly. "Can't talk. In a hurry. And don't let my dad catch you out here again."

Clod combed his hair with a gardening fork. "What? He doesn't like my *landscaping*?"

Ember gave a small chuckle but continued with her tasks.

"Anyway," continued Clod, "June Bloom is coming, and you just gotta be my date. 'Cause check it out, I'm all grown up!" He lifted his arm branch, revealing a flower growing from his armpit. "And I smell *gooooood!*"

He sniffed the flower before plucking it to hand to Ember. *Poof.* The moment Ember touched the blossom, it went up in flames.

"Sorry, buddy." Ember shrugged. "Elements don't mix."

"Come on!" Clod begged. "Go to the festival with me! You never leave this part of town."

"That's because everything I need is right here," Ember countered.

As they spoke, a high-speed train passed by on the elevated track that ran past Firetown, cascading water. Knowing exactly what to do, Ember popped open her umbrella, deflecting the deluge. She scowled as the train sped away. That bridge connecting her street to downtown Element City was the *only* source of water Firetown hadn't been able to get rid of.

"The city isn't made with Fire people in mind," Ember reminded Clod. "It would take an act of God to get me to cross that bridge."

"An act of God?" Clod raised his twiggy eyebrows. "Or an act of *Clod*?"

"Gotta run!"

Ember revved her scooter's engine and zipped off, leaving a trail of scorch marks behind her. She loved this part of her job—feeling her scooter bumping along on the cobblestone streets as she flew past fuel huts and smoke cleaners and kiosks selling fire-roasted wood. She relished the way the wind whipped through her flames, causing them to dance like blazing ribbons. Firetown was aglow with activity, and as she clocked stop after stop, she couldn't help feeling that her family's store was the center of it all.

With a screech, she skidded up just beside a couple pushing a charcoal grill down the sidewalk.

"As ordered!" She handed them a bottle of lighter fluid.

The mother lifted the lid off the grill, revealing a little Fire baby keeping warm. The baby grabbed the bottle and sucked it down in one gulp, burping flames.

A moment later, Ember peeled around a corner only to find herself stuck behind a slow-moving truck.

"Oh, come *on!*" she growled impatiently. With a burst of effort, she ignited her flame just enough to send her scooter up and over the truck. She shook an angry fist at the driver before zooming forward, one thought prevailing above all: breaking her àshfá's delivery record was something she *knew* she could do.

Tools to wood shops, spices to restaurants, firecrackers to street carts, and sandbags to construction workers. Everything a Fire community needed to thrive, the Fireplace could deliver.

As the sun set over their little corner of the city, Ember gazed up at the sky streaked with burning red and pink, and she wondered: how many more Fire people were out there in the world? Did they know this perfect haven made just for them existed? Did they know that her àshfá's dream had made it all possible?

It was growing dark by the time Ember's scooter rumbled back up to the Fireplace. The sign on the front window had been flipped to CLOSED, yet the timer on the counter was still ticking down. Ember gasped as she raced through the door. She had done it! She had beaten her àshfá's record!

"Winner winner, charcoal dinner!" she whooped, energized by her victory.

But her cheer was met by a snore, and she gasped quietly.

Her àshfá had fallen asleep by the register, surrounded by paperwork and red dot stickers in preparation for the next day's big sale.

Ember quietly tiptoed over and pulled a chainmail shawl over her father's shoulders. Her poor àshfá. He looked even older as he slept. The corners of Ember's mouth drooped with sadness. It was her fault her àshfá had to keep working so hard. When was she ever going to make this right?

Bernie startled awake, coughing out a little puff of smoke.

"Head to bed." Ember lovingly pulled a red dot sticker off his cheek. "I'll close things up."

Just then, the timer went off. Bernie rubbed his eyes groggily, making sense of what was happening.

"You beat my record?" he asked in awe.

Ember shrugged. "I learned from the best."

Bernie smiled warmly at his daughter, the two sharing a moment of celebration only they could understand.

Then he began coughing again, the puffs of smoke coming out darker than before. "I am old," he admitted. "I can't do this forever." He looked at Ember with an expression of raw clarity she rarely saw in his eyes. "Tomorrow I'll sleep in. And I want *you* to run the Red Dot Sale."

It took Ember a second to process what her àshfá had said. When his words finally registered, the warm radiance of elation spread across her face.

"Seriously? By myself?" she asked, scarcely daring to believe it.

Bernie nodded. "If you can do that without losing your temper, it will show me you are able to take over."

Ember hardly knew what to say. The culmination of . . . everything . . . finally happening when she wasn't even sure she believed it possible anymore.

Her voice breaking, she hugged her father tight. "You got it, Àshfá. I won't let you down. I swear. You'll see."

Chapter 10

"What was it this time, Wade?" Gale's puffs looked particularly disgruntled today, dark and brimming with little lightning sparks flickering here and there. As the sole Air person in charge of the city Citation Division, she'd heard a lot of hot-air excuses in her day. But never had she encountered more sob stories than from the department's newest city inspector, Wade Ripple.

"I couldn't help it," Wade blubbered, holding a soggy citation booklet in his hands. "The bamboo blossoms . . . they were so beautiful . . ."

"That doesn't mean any self-proclaimed green thumb can grow an unpermitted seed plot in their backyard!" Gale puffed, exasperated. "Bamboo blossoms are *invasive*, Wade. They spread like wildfire. Because of you, half of Green Village is overrun with vines!"

"But . . . so much beauty!" Wade burst into a waterfall of tears. Gale sighed.

"Wade, your heart's in the right place. But I'm going to be straight with you. You wouldn't even be here if I didn't owe your mom a favor. Her design instincts are flawless, but your work ethic isn't. You're a city inspector. That means you inspect the city *for* violations, and you *write them up*. As much as it pains me, I'm going to have to let you go if you keep giving every Element with a sob story a free pass."

"No!" Wade's expression flipped from sorrow to panic. "I can't lose another job—not after what happened at the construction site the other month."

"I know, I know," Gale said. "That's why I'm going to give you one more chance, kid." Gale whooshed up a fresh batch of citation notes and handed them to Wade. "Apparently, the city has a problem even bigger than bamboo blossoms that I need you to investigate. We've gotten reports of water leaking into some of the closed-up canals down by the river. That shouldn't be possible. Somewhere, something's broken. I want you to find the source of the leak and fix it. And if it's a violation of some kind, you *write it up*."

Wade's eyes grew wide. "But the city has thousands of canals. Where do I start?"

"I didn't say it would be easy." Gale puffed up and flew over her desk to start her day's paperwork. "But if you can handle this, you can keep the job. Got it?"

"Yes!" Wade saluted, splashing water all over Gale's desk. "I won't let you down, Gale sir—madam—Air boss lady!"

With a slosh, Wade turned and rushed out of the room. Gale looked down at her desk, let out a low thunder rumble, and began placing heavy paperweights on all the soggy documents. It was going to take a lot of air to blow this mess dry.

Days. Wade had been searching for days. And he was exactly zero percent closer to finding the source of the leak in Element City. He'd scoured every canal and culvert door from Green Village to the Peat Packing District, and he couldn't find any source of any leak anywhere.

"This is impossible." Wade wallowed to himself, sloshing along an empty canal that ran beside the river. "I'm never going to find it. And I don't even have anyone to talk to."

He gazed out at the river that separated downtown Element City from smoldering Firetown. The brick and stone buildings there glowed red in the early morning light, reflecting off the river's choppy waves.

"At least that's one part of the city I don't have to search," he mused. "No water over there." He wondered for a moment what Firetown was like—it wasn't a place he'd ever really visited. Not because it wasn't nice. But for as long as Wade could remember, Water folks just hadn't really flowed over into that section of the city. Someone had told him about the food there once—dishes so hot they could make your face boil. *What would that be like?* he wondered. *Would it burn? Or maybe just feel bubbly? Would you evaporate and not even realize it? Probably not that last one. Elements don't evaporate from spicy food. But still, imagine that. Taking a bite of . . . what were they called? . . . oh, yeah, kol nuts, and just starting to bubble so hot you turned to steam, and before you realized what was happening,* poof. *Gone! Just like that! What a sad way to go!*

"Oh my whirlpool," Wade suddenly said aloud. He'd been standing in the same spot for thirty minutes. "I don't believe it. I get distracted even by talking to *myself*. Gale is right! I really don't have what it takes to focus on this job!"

Wade puddled up into the canal. He loved a good cry, but sometimes he almost felt like he was out of tears to shed. If he was hopeless at every job, what else could he do?

"I'm adrift," he said sadly. "Just like Dad warned me."

Without meaning to, he felt himself spilling over and connecting to a nearby puddle at the side of the canal.

"Wait a second." He popped his head up. "This is a restricted canal. There shouldn't be any water here."

Re-forming, Wade dipped his finger into the puddle of water and tasted it. "Rusty." He smacked his lips curiously. "With a hint of motor oil?" He gasped. "Could this be it? Did I find it? Did I actually do something right?"

A wave of hope washed over him. Wade looked down the canal to see if there were any more clues about the water's source.

There was a clue. A big clue. And it was coming straight for him.

"Holy dewdrop!" Wade exclaimed. A huge rush of water was coming straight for him down the canal that was supposed to be empty!

"Ahhhhhh!" Wade tried to run, but it was no use. The water swept over him, churning him up and around and somersaulting him in a nauseating rush he wasn't sure he could escape.

Slurp! Helpless to stop it, Wade felt himself get sucked into the canal's old water filtration grate. Darkness engulfed him as he became hopelessly commingled with dirt and debris far beneath the city streets.

"I'm going to get trapped down here," Wade panicked amidst the chaos. "I'm going to be stuck forever! Heeeeeeelp!"

His words bubbled soundlessly in the flood. And surrounded by darkness, completely and utterly alone, Wade realized that this might, in fact, be the end of his drifting once and for all.

BAM!

Something exploded nearby. What was happening? As if getting trapped in an underground pipe system wasn't bad enough, was he going to get blown up, too?

With a rush, Wade felt himself getting sucked into another pipe by a massive force, and he whooshed along with the water, powerless to stop himself from heading wherever the current was taking him.

Chapter 11

Today was the day. The day Ember's life would change.

"No pressure," she said to herself, adjusting the Red Dot Sale pin affixed to her apron. So what if everything she'd been working toward for the past ten years all came down to this one epic sale? She totally had this under control. Just to be safe, she did a few high-knee jumps and squats to let off some steam. Then she stood still, breathing deeply, imagining the warm glow of pride she would feel by the end of a successful Red Dot Sale. Her mother and father would weep lava tears of joy as they packed their suitcases for a well-deserved holiday as Ember—the one and only Ember—waved to them from behind the register of her very own Fireplace.

Or—she couldn't keep the thought from creeping in—if things went poorly, the wretched disappointment she would feel knowing she'd blown her final shot, the years continuing to roll by as she watched her àshfá grow older and weaker behind the counter. Ember's own ambition would slowly snuff out and drift away.

"No!" She pushed the ugly thoughts away. "I've got this. Take a breath. Calm as a candle."

Ember rolled up the shade to the front window of the store.

"Oh, flame . . ." She gulped.

Standing outside was a packed crowd of Fire people, their fiery faces all pressed against the glass, waiting to bust in.

She sucked in her breath. "Here we go."

"Morning!" she greeted as she unlocked the door. "Welcome to the Firepl—"

The crowd trampled past, nearly crushing Ember in their mad dash to reach the red-stickered shelves.

"How much are these?"

"Are all the red stickers the same?"

"What does no sticker mean?"

"This one is damaged."

"Is everything final sale?"

Every time Ember tried to answer one question, someone else was right up in her face holding a stickered or un-stickered or, worse, freshly broken item.

Out of the corner of her eye, Ember noticed a customer yanking on a can of chunky lava soup at the bottom of a pyramid display.

"Whoa, whoa, whoa!" Ember rushed to keep him from toppling over the whole tower. "They're all the same." She handed him a can from the top and forced a grin. "Thanks for shopping!"

"Are these fragile?" a woman's voice rang out behind her just before . . .

Crash!

Ember winced. "Yes. They were."

Over by the register, a father was allowing his triplets to eat handfuls of hot logs straight from the display while he examined a red-stickered shovel.

"No, no, no!" Ember dashed forward and yanked the kids' hands away. The father glared at her, and she again forced a smile. "You have to pay before you eat," she explained.

Suddenly, the register was overrun with customers who wanted to check out. Right. Now.

"How much is this?"

"What's your return policy?"

"My dad broke this."

"Does this come in large?"

"Has anyone seen my husband?"

Ember breathed. And breathed. And breathed.

But the frustration boiling up inside her was just too intense. She was suffocating. She was turning purple.

"Mind if I test this kettle?" a customer called. The kettle whistled with a shrill pitch.

Ember was going to explode.

Covering her mouth with both hands and sparking purple, Ember streaked toward the back room. "Back in five minutes!" she shouted, muffled.

Away. She had to get away. Far away, where they couldn't see her when she popped. She couldn't keep it in!

The basement. Yes! She ran for the basement, slamming the iron door behind her and pelting down the stairs to the center of the room before—

"AHHHHHHHHHHHHHHHHH!!"

Ember exploded with fury, screaming with a primal rage that practically incinerated the air around her. Flames flew everywhere. No corner remained unscorched.

After a long, long moment, Ember finally stopped, panting, hands on her knees.

There. That was better. Just had to let it out. No harm done.

Rummmble.

Uh-oh.

Ember looked up with trepidation through the clearing smoke. A large black pipe on the edge of the room had taken the brunt of her explosion. It was cracked and rattling. And then . . .

FWOOM!

The pipe burst, shooting out streams of water everywhere!

"Oh, no!" Ember cried in panic.

The basement was filling up fast. She had to stop that leak—water couldn't be in the Fireplace! She grabbed a nearby umbrella and lunged for the pipe, her feet steaming in the deluge. Desperately, she forced the umbrella against the crack even as jets of water shot her in the face, stinging her cheeks and putting out bits of her shoulders. With a huge effort, she melted the leak shut. Phew. She had done it. The water leak stopped.

But Ember was a half-doused mess. Wincing, she hobbled over to some sticks that hadn't gotten soaked, and shoved them in her mouth all at once. Slowly, the pain subsided, and her flame was restored. Then she took in the damage.

"Oh, no." Everything in the basement was completely soaked. Sandbags. Logs. Wood parcels and fuel pellets. "Oh no, no, no, no, no. Stupid temper! Not today!"

What was she going to do? She had to clean this up, but all the customers were still waiting upstairs. It could be an all-out brawl up there by now, for all she knew. And she couldn't ask her parents for help, because that would mean admitting she had lost her temper. And *that* would snuff out any hopes of ever running the store for good. She had to fix this on her own. But look at this mess!

"What is wrong with me?" She held her head in her hands.

Through her flaming fingertips, she watched soiled supplies floating on the surface of the water. A ledger of prior years' sales. An upside-down bucket. Even a few keepsakes and photo frames, all destroyed.

Without warning, one of the picture frames began gliding along the surface as though something was pushing it. Then two streams of water bubbled up, accompanied by the sound of crying.

"What the—" Ember stared, completely confused.

Before her very eyes, a Water man re-formed up and out from the pool, bawling his eyes out. Though Ember had no way of knowing, it was none other than Wade Ripple.

"What a happy family!" the man sobbed, pointing to the photo. It happened to be a snapshot of Ember celebrating her fifth birthday with her parents. "Is that your *dad*? I love dads! And it's your *birthday*!"

"Who are you?" Ember yelped, jumping back. "What are you doing here?"

"I don't know!" the intruder lamented, looking around the room like he was trying to figure out where he was. "I was searching for a leak on the other side of the river, and I got sucked in! Ohhh . . . this is bad. I can't lose another job! I just can't seem to find my flow."

Ember couldn't believe what she was seeing. What was this guy doing here? Why was a Water person even in Firetown?

And how had he gotten so . . . chiseled? Despite her confusion, Ember couldn't help noticing the Water guy's many rippling muscles. Usually, only rock Earth Elements could achieve that sort of sculpting. Whoever this guy was, he must have worked out. A lot.

"Dang," Ember said.

The man noticed Ember studying him and glanced down at his own body. "Ugh, that pipe squished me all out of shape." He jostled his water around a bit, allowing the "muscles" of his chest to flop back down to his belly where they belonged so he looked normal again. "That's better."

Snapping back to herself, Ember flared. "Dude, just get out of here! I've got to clean this mess before my dad sees what I did."

"Oooh, actually . . ." The man sloshed over to the cracked pipe and examined the burn marks around the makeshift garbage lid patch. "I'm afraid I'm going to have to write you a citation."

Ember furrowed her brow. "A citation?"

"Yeah." The man nodded dutifully. "I'm a city inspector. And this pipe is definitely not up to code."

Ember felt like she was going to go purple again. "I sucked a city inspector into our pipes?!"

"I know. Ironic, right?" The guy began poking the pipe.

"Stop messing with that!" Ember shouted, not wanting the crack to burst open again.

"I need to make sure it's solid," the inspector insisted.

"Oh, it's solid." Ember folded her arms. "I should know. My dad built it himself. Every brick and board. This place was a ruin when he found it."

The inspector's eyes widened as he gazed around the room as though seeing it anew. "Wow. He did all this himself?" His eyes filled with watery tears. "*Without* permits?"

"Uh . . ." Ember gulped.

"Oh!" The inspector sobbed. "I'm going to have to write that up, too! First I'm sucked into a pipe, and now I have to write citations that could get this place shut down. Oh, gosh. It's just too much!"

The purple drained from Ember's cheeks as her fire ran cold. "Shut us *down*?"

"I know! It's awful!" the inspector wailed, ripping a completed citation from his booklet.

"No!" Ember begged. "You can't shut us down. Please! This is a big day for me. It's our Red Dot Sale!" She lunged for the citation papers. But the Water man easily flowed out of the way.

"Hey, take it easy!" he exclaimed. "This is as hard on me as it is on you! I gotta get these to City Hall before the end of my shift."

Before she could stop him, the inspector streamed up and out through the basement window. Furious, Ember pushed it open, watching the Water man re-form in the dry canal outside the building and start heading toward the elevated train platform.

"Flame!" This was a complete disaster! Now what was she supposed to do? The Red Dot Sale pin on her apron was a nasty reminder of all the customers waiting upstairs. Angry. Unsupervised. Probably having a free-for-all. But she couldn't let that inspector get away with the citations. If she didn't stop him, there wouldn't *be* a store to hold a Red Dot Sale in anymore. All because of her stupid temper!

This was her mess to fix. And she wasn't going down without a fight!

Chapter 12

Wade felt sorry for that young Fire woman at the store. He really did. He hadn't *meant* to flow into her basement. He still didn't even know how that had happened. It was lucky for him he'd made it out of the pipe at all. One minute, it felt like he was trapped. The next, he was floating in a pool of water looking up at a warm glowing light. For a second there, he wondered if all those old stories were true and that when you reached the afterlife, you found yourself "heading toward the light." But this light had looked kind of sad. That was when he realized it wasn't a mysterious light at all but a Fire person. A kind of pretty one, too. Until he made her angry.

You were just doing your job, Wade told himself sternly as he rode the jostling train back over the river toward downtown

Element City. *I don't want that shop to get in trouble. But I also can't get fired again!*

The train entered a tunnel, casting everything in shadow. *I'm sure they'll be fine,* Wade tried to convince himself, though the tears welling behind his eyes threatened to drip on the train floor and make everything slippery. He took a wobbly breath. Happy thoughts. He needed happy thoughts. *She said her dad had repaired the store before with his own two hands! I'm sure they can do it again! And you know what? When they reopen, I'll be their first customer. Maybe I'll even try some kol nuts. I've always wondered if they really do make your water boil.*

"Next stop, City Hall," a voice over the loudspeaker announced. But Wade wasn't paying attention. He was so lost in his own thoughts about kol nuts and the Fire shop that he could almost feel his hand bubbling.

Wait a second . . . his hand *was* bubbling.

"Ah!" Wade yelped and looked down with a start. The Fire woman from the shop was crouched next to him, her light shielded by a hooded cloak. She had followed him! And she was reaching for the citations in his hand, making his water boil with her heat!

"Hands off!" he exclaimed.

Whipping his hand away, Wade squished between people on the train and pushed his way out through the opening doors onto the City Hall Station platform. He had to get these citations to his supervisor before that Fire girl could try to snatch them away again. Didn't she understand? He was just doing his job!

Wade rushed down the station stairs and out onto the busy street, glancing nervously behind to see if she was following.

She *was* following him! And she could *move*. It looked almost like she was parkouring down the stairs after him, the way she kept bouncing off things to propel herself forward. She even ninja-bounced off a lamppost!

Oh—oh, no. No, wait. She wasn't parkouring. She was tumbling down the stairs, completely out of control. But despite her stylish free fall, she was still gaining on him. He had to get out of here!

Wade looked ahead and sprinted. He made it all the way to the end of the block, where a nursery school bus was letting out a group of children. *Aw, look at all those cute little faces.* Wade slowed down a tiny bit to wave to all the happy Earth kids.

Ack! The woman used her umbrella like a hot-air balloon, warming the air underneath it and floating over the children! Wade zipped left down an alleyway and out of sight. Thinking fast, he squished into a space between two apartment buildings that was only a few inches wide. If she couldn't see him, she couldn't follow him.

"I think I lost her," Wade thought desperately as he pushed forward.

An intense heat grew behind him.

Nope—she had found him! Now she was squishing between the buildings, too, right on his tail!

"Come on." Wade breathed hard. He just needed to make it to the other side of these buildings. City Hall was right there. If he reached it, he could simply send the citations up the delivery tube, his job would be done, and he wouldn't be fired. With a surge of effort, he popped out from between the two buildings and into the sunlight. City Hall was only a few yards away. He'd made it—

"Holy hot sauce!"

The woman leapt in front of him, holding a bottle of oil she'd swiped from a Dirt Burger street vendor. Her eyes burning, she sprayed a circle of oil around herself and ignited into a flaming wall of apocalyptic rage.

"Come on, guy," she panted through gritted teeth. "You can't get through this. So it's time to hand 'em over."

Wade looked at the fiery adversary before him. Then down at his feet at a drainage grate in the sidewalk.

"Oh, boy. I'm sorry," he said. He really meant it. "This is going to be really disappointing for you."

With one fluid step, Wade slipped down into the drainage grate, flowed through the drain to the other side of the sidewalk, and popped back up in front of the City Hall entrance.

"No, no, no, no, no!" he heard the woman calling behind him. "Please! No! You don't understand!"

But he had no choice. This was his job. He marched through the revolving doors, placed the citations into a metal canister, and sent them through the vacuum tube, and suddenly . . .

"Whoa." The wall in front of Wade shone with thousands of refracted light sparkles. It was like a rainbow of diamonds twinkling before him. He turned and realized that the light was coming from the Fire woman. A prism of colors, glowing not with rage but with surreal, transfixing beauty.

"The shop is my dad's dream," the woman said quietly, vulnerable, more to herself than to Wade. "If I'm the reason it gets shut down, it will kill him. He will never trust me to take over."

Oh, man. Now Wade felt *terrible*. If there was one thing that tugged right at his heartstrings, it was stories about dads. He exited the building and walked toward the woman.

"Why didn't you say that before?" Wade asked.

The young woman looked up hopefully. "Does that mean you'll tear up the tickets?"

"I mean, I would . . ." Wade hesitated. "But I just sent them over to the processing department."

The woman fumed again, her prismatic light vanishing.

"Whoa! Whoa!" Wade held up his hands in mock surrender.

"Maybe there's something I can do." Wade racked his brain. How could he help the Fire woman *without* getting fired?

"Oh!" he said, having a sudden thought bubble. "What if I take you over there to plead your case? That could work!"

The woman hesitated for a moment before curtly nodding her head.

"Phew." Wade sighed as he led her into the building. This "doing his job" business got a little heated sometimes.

"So what's your name?" he asked as they walked down the long hallway.

"Ember," she said shortly.

"My name's Wade," he said. "Nice to officially meet you! It's kind of funny how we met, when you think about it. I mean, I'm a city inspector who got sucked through a pipe that just happened to be in violation of city code. And you're a shopkeeper who just happens to want to make her dad proud, the way I always wanted to make my dad proud. Feels like it could be straight out of a movie. Funny, right?"

"Hysterical," Ember replied.

A few moments later, Wade ushered Ember into the familiar jungle office of Fern Grouchwood, the city citation coordinator. Wade was used to the humid atmosphere and lush foliage the old Earth employee kept in his office. But Ember seemed unsettled, holding her arms stiffly at her sides like she was afraid of touching anything.

"Hey, Fern!" Wade greeted him. "How you doing?"

"Living the dream," Fern answered in his drawling voice.

"You know those citations I just gave you from Firetown?" Wade asked.

Fern held up the metal canister with the citations inside. "I was about to send them to Mrs. Cumulus and then get sprayed for fungus rot."

"Before you do, maybe she could have a word?" Wade asked hopefully. He nodded to Ember, who stepped forward, still looking awkward.

"Hi," Ember said with an overwide smile. She leaned on the desk, and a stack of paperwork instantly burst into flames.

"Whoa!" She laughed nervously, then turned to Fern. "Look, I know that we have some non-permitted stuff in our shop." She winked. "But who doesn't skate around permits sometimes?"

Fern raised a leafy eyebrow. "You do realize you're saying this, out loud, to the actual permit office, right?" He moved to put the canister in one of the vacuum tubes.

"Wait!" Wade interrupted. "Tell him what you told me," he whispered to Ember. "About your dad and letting him down."

"No," Ember replied. "That's too personal."

But Wade didn't get it. Wasn't it worse to let her dad down than to not talk about it?

"Her dad will be super disappointed," Wade said to Fern on Ember's behalf.

"Stop!" Ember said anxiously.

But Fern had turned to Wade, looking interested in the story. Now was their chance!

"He might even be *ashamed.*" Wade nodded meaningfully. Fern knew Wade's history with his own dad. The Earth supervisor was all leaf ears. Maybe they would get those citations ripped up after all!

"What are you doing?" Ember whispered fiercely behind him, her cheeks glowing purple with what Wade assumed was embarrassment.

"But the main thing is if her father can't retire . . ." Wade pressed on.

"Stop. Talking." Ember's voice sounded strange. Was she getting hotter?

"It would be all Ember's fauuuuu—YEOW!"

Without warning, Ember exploded in a giant ball of fire! Wade's water boiled. He even steamed a little. And all the citations on Fern's desk went up in a massive *whoosh* of singed ash. All except

Ember's citations, which were still safely tucked inside the metal canister.

"Looks like I'm going home early today," Fern said in his drawling voice, any interest in Ember's story evaporated. With a *thwoop*, he popped the citations into the processing tube. "Expect to be shut down within a week. Have a good one."

Wade looked sadly at Ember, who was breathing heavily, her expression hard to read. She looked almost shocked at her own fire force. And . . . scared?

What a shame. Wade shook his head. He had tried hard to help.

But as Wade knew well, sometimes it was harder to listen.

Chapter 13

Ember trudged the long, woeful way back home. She couldn't believe everything that had happened in just the past few hours. First the Red Dot Sale fiasco. Then the basement flood. And now the entire Fireplace was probably going to get shut down. All because of her.

How was she ever going to tell her àshfá?

As she rounded a corner, the sight she currently dreaded most came into view: the Fireplace. Where she would have no choice but to own up to everything. This was, without a doubt, the worst day of her life.

But as she got closer, her fire flickered with a fresh wave of worry. There were no customers milling around, and the sign on the front door was flipped to CLOSED. But it was only lunchtime!

Full-on panicking, Ember flew into the shop.

"Hello?" she called frantically.

Her àshfá coughed down in the basement, and Ember sprinted for the stairs. When she reached the bottom, her hand flew to her mouth.

"Oh, no!"

Pipes were cracked and leaking everywhere! Her parents were desperately working to repair the damage, barely avoiding being doused themselves.

"Dad!" shouted Ember.

"Ember!" Bernie looked up in relief at his daughter's arrival.

"What happened?" Ember exclaimed as she raced over to help her parents melt the cracks closed.

"We're lucky nobody was hurt!" Bernie fumed. "It ruined the Red Dot Sale!"

Ember winced. Here it came—the fallout.

"Did *he* do this?" Bernie asked angrily.

"Who?" Ember asked, confused.

"That Water guy I saw you chase!"

"Oh . . . uh . . ." Ember hesitated. She hadn't realized her àshfá had seen her chasing Wade. She knew she should own up to the truth. But instead . . .

"Yeah, he did. He just broke through a pipe." Ember heard the words coming out of her mouth before she'd even decided to say them. "I don't know why. Luckily, I was able to close it off. I, uh, couldn't catch him, though."

At that, her father flared. "Water! Always trying to water us down!"

"He was a Water *person*, Dad," Ember corrected him, never feeling comfortable when her àshfá used that sort of talk. "Not just water."

But Bernie persisted. "Same thing! And why is there water in the pipes? The city shut it down years ago! There should be no water!" Overheated with aggravation, Bernie collapsed into a coughing fit, stumbling toward the damp floor.

"Dad!" Ember caught him before he could touch the water. She and her mother carried him to the safe, dry stairway, where he struggled to regain his breath.

"We will get through this." Cinder rubbed his back soothingly, helping calm his burning anger. "Just like before."

"Before?" Ember looked up. "Before what?" Had the basement flooded a time that she didn't know about?

But her parents exchanged looks that told Ember they weren't talking about the basement.

Slowly, Bernie nodded, and Cinder turned to Ember. "There is a reason we left Fire Land."

Ember grew very still. Her parents *never* talked about Fire

Land. She suddenly felt a bit scared about what they were going to reveal.

Cinder's gaze grew distant as she thought back to a long-ago memory. "Oh, Ember. It was so beautiful there. Here in Firetown, we are the only family with a Blue Flame. But back home, every family had one."

"What happened?" Ember asked.

"We had a shop," Cinder said with a sad smile. "A beautiful shop. Your father put everything we had into that dream. But the winds in Fire Land are unforgiving. The day we were supposed to open, a fierce storm hit. We just managed to rescue our Blue Flame before the winds ripped through. The storm was over in a matter of moments, but our shop—it was gone. Years of work reduced to rubble. All was lost for us, and I was already pregnant with you. That was when we decided we must leave."

"But why?" Ember asked. "Why not rebuild in Fire Land? Just because one storm hit didn't mean another would."

Cinder shook her head. "That is what your father's parents wanted. But we knew—we couldn't go through that again. Wondering each day if another windstorm would take everything away from us. We didn't want to live with that fear. We needed to start over somewhere new."

Cinder glanced at Bernie. "His parents did not understand.

They were upset. It was the last time your father ever saw his family. But we had such hope that Element City could give us what Fire Land couldn't. A safe place to grow and opportunities that wouldn't be snuffed out. That is why we came here. To build this. Our new life."

Throughout the whole story, Ember's àshfá kept his gaze focused on the puddled floor. The hurt from these memories had dulled his flame's color to a subdued rust. Ember wasn't used to seeing him this quiet.

Eventually, Bernie got to his feet and shakily collected a mop to continue cleaning without a word. It made Ember feel very, very sad.

She walked over and grasped the top of the handle to slow his work, holding his gaze.

"Àshfá . . . *nothing* will happen to this shop or the flame again. I promise." Ember's resolve burned to her very core.

Bernie touched his palm to her cheek. "Mm," he said simply. "Good daughter."

Chapter 14

The sound waves from pulsing music vibrated through Wade's headphones, gently rippling his face. He loved this time of day. The streets were quiet as he walked to work. The sun was just rising, striating the distant cloud apartments with peaceful pink hues. These were the perfect meditative moments for Wade to be alone with his thoughts. No worries about citations or getting fired to interrupt his—

"YEOW! Fire!" He had almost stepped on what looked like a burning pile of clothes right outside the entrance to his office! He started to stamp out the flames when, inexplicably, they moved.

"Hey! HEY!" The fire stood up, revealing it had been Ember huddled up by the door all along.

"Oh!" Wade exclaimed in surprise. "Sorry! You're just so hot!"

"Excuse me?" Ember raised an eyebrow.

"No!" Wade hurried to explain himself. "I mean like you're smokin'! No, wait—I didn't mean—ugh."

"Are you done yet?" Ember asked.

Wade hung his head, dripping with embarrassment. "Yes, please."

Ember sat back down. "I'm waiting to talk to your boss. So make like a stream and . . . flow somewhere else."

"Actually, Gale won't be in today," Wade told her. "She's a huge airball fan, and the Windbreakers are finally in the playoffs. Toot, toot!"

Wade did an impression of the Windbreakers' team cheer. But the news was not welcome to Ember.

"UGH!" She flared up in frustration.

Wade flinched. Boy, she sure got heated up over everything! Still, he had to admire her determination to wait outside first thing in the morning to try to change something that was important to her. Ember had spunk, that was for sure.

"Okay . . ." he said after a long pause. "Well, I just came by because I left my passes for the game here last night." He started to head inside, but Ember's fire suddenly flickered a bright golden, catching his eye.

"Passes?" she asked. "Like, plural?"

Ember had never been inside an airball stadium. She had never been inside *any* stadium. Fire sports were usually well-grounded and outdoors. But Cyclone Stadium, as Wade had called it, was . . . incredible. Ember never knew something like this even existed in Element City. Towering rows of seats soared hundreds of feet into the air, each holding enthusiastic fans wearing jerseys for either the home team, the Windbreakers, or the visiting opponents, the Cropdusters. Higher above still floated the airball players, huffing and puffing and whooshing around the arena as they battled to blow a billowy airball into one of two hoops. To Ember, it all seemed so—light. She couldn't imagine floating like that, free to glide as high as you pleased, high enough to touch the sun.

"So where's Gale?" she asked Wade.

"Up there, in that skybox." Wade pointed to a private box high above and to the right. Ember squinted, then gulped. Gale was a very grumpy-looking Air person. Her cloud body was lumpy, dark, and gray, with little streaks of lightning arcing as she shouted from her seat.

"C'mon, Windbreakers! BREAK SOME WIND!"

"Okay." Ember steeled herself. "Time to cancel some tickets."

As she and Wade passed through tightly squeezed rows of fans, Ember realized it wasn't just Air Elements who came to these games. Many Water and Earth fans were mixed in as well, all wearing jerseys. The only Element conspicuously not among the crowd was Fire.

Except for Ember.

"Excuse me. Sorry. Pardon me. Fire girl coming through." She carefully edged her way through, several fans giving her nasty looks as she accidentally boiled their water or singed their leaves.

"Jimmy, what's up?" Wade called to one spectator. "Wendy! How good is it to be here?" he said to another.

Ember rolled her eyes. Of course Wade would know everyone here.

They finally reached Gale's box. The cloud supervisor looked even darker and stormier up close.

"Hi, Gale!" Wade greeted her. "How you doing?"

"Look at that score!" Gale gestured angrily toward the scoreboard, which showed the Windbreakers were trailing by many points. "What do you think?" She rumbled as she shouted out to the players, "Blow the *ball*, not the *game*!"

Ember stood hesitantly off to the side. But Wade motioned to her, and she inched toward his boss.

"Yeah . . . so, uh, Gale. My name is Ember Lumen. My family runs a Fire shop. Wade wrote us a bunch of tickets yesterday, and—"

The buzzer sounded and Gale erupted, blowing back Ember's and Wade's faces with a gust. "WHAT KIND OF CALL WAS THAT?!" She eyed Ember as her lightning sizzled down. "Lumen? Yeah, Fire shop with thirty citations."

"Thirty?" Ember shot Wade a nasty glance, and he shrugged apologetically.

"Anyway, friend"—Ember turned back to Gale—"I was hoping we could work something out."

The buzzer went off again and the home team crowd booed. The Windbreakers had lost another point even though the Cropdusters had fouled several players.

"Come on, ref!" Gale fluffed up in a fury. "ARE YOUR EYES IN THE BACK OF YOUR HEAD?!"

The Air referee's eyes literally popped to the back of his head to glare at Gale.

"Yeah, bummer," Ember said, not really getting why Gale was so whirled up by one dumb point. "Okay, so, the thirty citations—"

"Do you mind?" Gale huffed. "There's a game going on." Then she muttered to herself, "Fireball."

That sparked Ember's ire.

"Actually, I *do* mind." Ember stepped in front of Gale, blocking her view. "This is my *life* we're talking about. Not some *game*."

" 'Some game'?" Gale's thunder rumbled. "This is the playoffs! So forgive me if I don't want to hear a sob story about the problems of some little shop."

Ember's fire blazed purple. "That 'little shop' matters way more than a bunch of overpaid cloud puffs blowing some ball around."

Despite the ongoing turmoil in the airball arena behind her, whether she wanted it or not, Ember now had Gale's full attention.

"I dare you." Gale floated nose to nose with Ember. "Say 'cloud puffs' one more time."

Ember emphasized each syllable. "Cloud. Puffs."

But before either of them could argue another word, Wade burst out behind them.

"Oh, no!"

An airball player with the name Lutz airbrushed onto his jersey had just missed the ball, allowing a crushing triple-point score by the Cropdusters. Gale's attention snapped back to the game, momentarily diverted from Ember's stinging insult.

"GAHH!" she screamed. "C'mon, Lutz! Get it together!"

"Lutz, man," Wade explained woefully to Ember, "he's been in such a funk because his mom has been sick."

The entire stadium booed, and Lutz's shoulders sagged.

"That is so not cool!" Wade insisted. "He's doing his best!"

With a sudden surge of energy, Wade stood up and shouted at the top of his lungs. "WE LOVE YOU, LUTZ!"

Surrounding fans looked at Wade like he was crazy. But undeterred, Wade motioned for everyone to start a chant. "C'mon! Say it with me! We love you, Lutz! We love you, Lutz!"

A small group of Water boys began splash-clapping. "We love you, Lutz! We love you, Lutz!"

Their parents joined in.

Followed by the row.

Followed by the section.

And before Ember's astonished eyes, the entire stadium joined in the chant.

"WE LOVE YOU, LUTZ! WE LOVE YOU, LUTZ!"

In the middle of the arena, Lutz looked at Wade and Ember's section gratefully, his cloud puffing out a bit more than before.

Then something even more incredible happened.

Wade started an *actual* wave.

"Whoooaaa . . ." he shouted.

"Whoooaaa!" echoed the crowd.

Ember opened her umbrella just in time as a wave of water splashed over their row, soaking Air, Earth, and Water Elements alike. She had never seen anything like this.

Energized, Lutz stole back the ball from the opposing team and smashed it into the hoop with astonishing speed.

"YEAH!" The crowd erupted into raucous cheers.

And without meaning to, Ember found herself cheering along with them.

Twenty home-team scores and an unbelievable Windbreaker win later, Ember, Gale, and Wade strode out of the stadium along with thousands of elated fans.

"What a comeback!" Gale whooped, her cloud cheerful and fluffy now.

"I've got to admit, that *was* pretty cool." Ember couldn't stop smiling.

"You can see why I get all churned up." Gale puffed happily. Then she eyed Ember. "But as a 'cloud puff' who used to come here with her dad, these wins mean a little bit more. And I really needed the win."

Ember realized that this was her shot. "And as a 'fireball' who's supposed to take over her dad's shop . . ." She paused before letting her guard down and going for it. "I sure don't want to let him down. I could use a win, too."

Gale nodded, seeming to understand. At her side, Wade also gave a nod of approval.

"Now I've just got to stop the water from coming in," Ember added.

"Hold the storm!" Gale choked, a tiny bit of lightning arcing in surprise. "*Water?* In *Firetown?*"

"Umm, yeah?" Ember said uneasily.

"Water was shut off there *years* ago!" Gale exclaimed. "Forget the tickets. I'm going to have to take apart your dad's shop to figure out what's going on!"

For the second time in two days, Ember's fire ran cold. "No—*you can't!* My dad put his *whole life* into that place!"

But Gale was clearly distracted by this new revelation. "Argh! I bet this is connected to that fluffin' leak!"

Ember looked to Wade desperately. What was Gale talking about?

"We've been trying to track down a leak in the city," Wade explained. "It's why I was in the canal, and—WAIT!" He gasped. "I know where I got sucked into Ember's shop! If these things *are* connected, Ember and I could track the water from her shop to find the source of the leak. I could call in a city crew to fix whatever we find!"

"Yes!" Ember jumped on board. "And there'd be no need to touch my dad's shop!"

Ember and Wade held their breath as Gale considered this. Finally, she seemed to de-puff a little, relaxing. She smiled at them. "You're lucky you're a cute couple."

"Huh?" Ember asked, confused. "Oh, no—we're not—"

"You've got until Friday," Gale stopped her. "If you can find the leak and get a crew to fix it by then, those citations are forgiven. If not? Your dad's shop gets shut down."

Chapter 15

Later that night, Ember and Wade peeked in through the windows of the Fireplace, watching as Ember's father desperately tried to repair pipes.

"Now the water is upstairs!" Bernie was complaining to Cinder. "I fix one pipe, and another one leaks!"

Ember looked at Wade, her eyes filled with worry. "How could it be worse?"

"Now that water's back, the pressure is forcing it up to all the pipes," Wade reasoned.

"We've got to find the source of that leak," Ember said. But even as she spoke, the sheer impossibility of the task before them overwhelmed her. "But how? We're searching for water *some-where* in a canal. And those canals go everywhere! Where do we even start?"

"It's why tracking down that leak has been so dang hard," Wade agreed.

Ember sighed, racking her brain. *Come on, Ember. Think!* There had to be a way to streamline their search. A way to get a clearer view of the problem . . .

Wade's watery head reflected the full moonlight, and Ember looked up to the night sky.

"The roof," she murmured.

A few moments later, Wade found himself on the roof of the Fireplace with Ember. The view from up here sure was pretty: all of Firetown twinkled below, like crimson crystals crisscrossing in an intricate city landscape.

"But we're not high enough," Wade pointed out as Ember grabbed a tarp off a nearby chimney cap. "We can't see all the canals from up here."

Ignoring him, Ember heaved the chimney cap off the brick smokestack and flipped it upside down. With an effort, she welded the tarp's metal hooks to the edges, creating a mock basket with a tarp attached. Then she heated the air under the tarp, pushing it upward like a hot-air balloon!

"Holy dewdrop!" Wade exclaimed. Ember wasn't just spunky; she was clever. And resourceful! Wade wouldn't ever have thought of making something like that.

"That is *so* cool!" he gushed.

"Shhh!" Ember clambered into the basket. "Get in!"

Soon the pair was floating high above Element City, observing the entire canal system from their own personal bird's-eye view.

"There!" Wade pointed to a pool of water far below in a canal that was supposed to be empty near the river's edge. "That's where I got sucked in. And look—more water!"

A trail of puddles stretched down the canal, like a line leading them through a maze.

"Go that way!" Wade pointed east, and Ember pushed them in the right direction, a lone spot of light shining against the dark night sky.

As he stood beside Ember, Wade enjoyed the warmth from her glow. She was so . . . determined. He really liked that about her. He knew she could get heated, but that was because she was passionate about the things she cared about. And the way her fire blazed sure was beautiful.

Ember must have sensed him watching her, because she glanced his way. Embarrassed to be caught staring, Wade pretended to admire the night sky.

"So, uh, what do you do at the shop, if you don't mind me asking?" Wade ventured the question.

"My dad's retiring, and I'll be taking over," Ember said. "Someday, when I'm ready."

"It must be nice knowing what you're going to do." Wade ruefully thought back on his long stream of workplace mishaps. "After my dad passed, I got all 'What's the point?' Now I just go from one job to the next."

Ember's glow changed beside him. A little softer, more rose-hued.

"There's a word in Firish," she told Wade. "*Tishók*'. It means 'embrace the light while it burns, because it won't always last forever.'"

Wade thought about that. What a nice way of putting it. And kind of sad.

"*Tee shook,*" he repeated quietly, getting the pronunciation completely wrong.

Ember smiled and shook her head. "Or something like that."

Just then, their balloon rounded a tall building, revealing a breathtaking view of the old section of Element City. Both Ember and Wade gasped. It was unbelievable. Rustic windmills dotted the landscape between original stone buildings constructed in the metropolis's founding days. Wade had never seen the city from this perspective. Clearly Ember hadn't, either, because her eyes were wide with wonder.

Then her face fell. Wade followed her gaze. She seemed to be staring at a large ornate building.

"You okay?" he asked.

"Yeah," Ember replied quietly.

"You sure?"

Ember sighed. "It's just, that building over there." She pointed to the building. "That's Garden Central Station. When I was a kid, my dad took me there because they had a Vivisteria tree—the only plant with flowers that can thrive in any environment. Fire included. I always wanted to see one." Ember paused, reliving the memory. "I was so excited. But they said our fire was too dangerous, and they wouldn't let us in. My dad was so angry and embarrassed." She paused again, perhaps reflecting on the gravity of her long-ago revelation.

Ember brushed her cheek bitterly. "The building flooded a few years later. So I missed my one chance to see a Vivisteria."

The whole time Ember spoke, Wade listened quietly, tears welling up with compassion. What a horrible thing for a little kid to go through. To be told you weren't the same as everyone else. He couldn't even imagine facing something like that.

"You must have been *so* scared," he said.

Ember looked at him in surprise. "Yeah. I was."

Her glowing eyes locked with his watery ones for a moment before she broke the connection. "Ugh. How do you do that?"

"Do what?" Wade asked, confused.

"Draw people in!" Ember flared a little. "You got a whole stadium to connect with you. I can't even connect with *one* customer. My stupid temper always kicks in."

Wade shrugged. "I guess I just say what I feel."

Ember scoffed and rolled her eyes a little.

"And I don't think a temper is so bad," Wade added. "Sometimes, when I lose my temper, I think it's just *me* trying to tell me something I'm not ready to hear."

"That's ridiculous," Ember huffed.

Something in Ember's tone resonated with Wade. She sounded angry, but Wade suspected she wasn't *actually* angry. In fact, it reminded him of the way he used to snap back at his dad whenever he suggested Wade play waveball or do waterworking or something Wade didn't think he'd ever be as good as his dad at. She sounded defensive. What was she protecting herself from?

"Maybe . . ." Wade started slowly.

But before he could finish, something below caught his eye. Something broken. The exact something they were looking for.

"Put us down there!" he exclaimed.

Chapter 16

Ember landed the balloon just outside a set of giant culvert doors in a puddle-strewn canal. The doors were old and worn, having been installed years before to close off that section of the system from the main canal. But they stood slightly ajar, no longer watertight.

Wade dipped his finger in a puddle and tasted the water. "Motor oil! Yup, this is the source!"

They walked through the doors into the spillover trough, which was completely empty.

"Why is there no water in here?" Ember asked.

"Because the doors are broken," Wade realized. "This is supposed to catch the spillover from those main canals, but because the doors are broken, it's leaking through into the sections that were meant to be closed off. We need to—RUN FOR OUR LIVES!"

A giant cruise ship had just passed by, sending a deluge of water surging over the spillover wall—straight for Ember and Wade!

The pair sprinted as fast as they could to safety. Ember leapt up onto some rebar attached to the culvert door, out of the way of the water. But Wade got caught in the current and gripped the edge of the door for dear life.

"Ahhh! Help!" he gurgled, being dragged down by the force.

Thinking fast, Ember melted a piece of rebar from the door and held it out to Wade, stretching as far as she could reach. "Quick! Grab this!"

Wade snatched the end of the metal bar, and Ember heaved with all her might. She just barely dragged Wade to safety as the massive current of water swept down the canal, pouring into the drainage pipes that led straight for . . .

"Firetown!" Ember gasped. They had to stop any more water from coming through—and fast!

Ember desperately looked around for something she could patch the crack between the doors with. Metal? A stone? She would have evaporated the water if she could, but there was too much.

Flaring her fire bright, she illuminated the shadows of the culvert and spotted a pile of sandbags stacked tall on the hill just beside the spillover.

"Hurry!" Ember scurried up to where the sandbags were and started tossing them down. "Help me!"

The deluge wasn't as powerful now, but water was still gushing through the doors. One by one, Ember tossed sandbags down to Wade, and he pushed them against the opening.

Then, to her amazement, Wade concentrated and pressed his undulating arm against the gush of water . . . connecting with it. It looked almost as though his arm became one with the spill-over. With a mighty effort, he forced the water back, willing it into the spillover area behind the culvert doors, giving him just enough time to shove several sandbags against the crack with his free arm.

"Whoa." Ember stopped without meaning to. Wade might not be chiseled. But he was strong.

"Ember, throw me more!" Wade called.

Working in tandem, Ember and Wade stacked bag after bag of sand against the doors until, finally, the water flow ceased, and the spillover began filling up as it was intended to.

Panting, Ember leaned on her knees and caught her breath. "So, will this hold?"

"I think so." Wade nodded, also breathing hard. "Until Friday, at least. By then I can get this great city crew to fix it."

Ember took another few deep breaths and collected her thoughts. This was good. For the time being, they had this thing fixed. Which meant her àshfá's shop was safe.

Which meant, maybe, she had done something right.

Ember looked up to Wade appreciatively . . . and realized there was an awkward glob of sand floating right in his face.

"Uh . . ." She stared.

"What?" Wade asked.

"You've got a little . . . sand."

"Oh." Wade's water reflected pink with embarrassment in Ember's glow. "Here?" He poked the opposite cheek from the sand glob.

"No—" Ember reached for his cheek but stopped, almost forgetting that they couldn't touch. "Just there."

Wade reached inside and pulled the clump of sand out. "Ah! Thanks."

"No problem." Ember held his gaze for a second longer than she intended. It was funny. Just minutes earlier, Wade had been battling back a deluge of water with a force like the ocean to help her. And now he was just kind of . . . normal. Like her. Something about him made her feel . . . she couldn't exactly explain it. Important? Vulnerable? A little bit of both?

"Okay, well." Ember broke the connection. "Let me know when it's done, I guess?"

She gave an awkward wave and turned to walk away. Then, suddenly, Wade called out, "Any chance you're free tomorrow to hang out with a Water guy?"

Ember turned and raised an eyebrow. "With a Water guy? My dad would boil you alive."

"He doesn't have to know!" Wade insisted. "We could meet in the city?"

Ember shook her head, but she was smiling. Why was she smiling?

"Sorry. That's not going to happen."

But Wade danced around excitedly.

"Ooh! You smiled! I saw it! Tomorrow. I'll be at the Alkali Theater. Three o'clock!"

Chapter 17

Wade shuffled nervously outside the theater. It was 3:02 p.m., but there was no sign of Ember. He glanced up at the marquee. *Tide and Prejudice* was starting soon. But he wasn't really worried about seeing the movie. He probably wouldn't even go if Ember didn't join him. He just kept hoping he would spot her fiery light coming down the sidewalk.

I know I saw her smile, he told himself. *But maybe something came up at her dad's shop? Or maybe the train is running late? What if she got food poisoning but she doesn't have my number and she can't call to tell me? Splashes and buckets, I should have given her my number!*

Wade looked hopefully across the street at the Elements all bustling this way and that. Water. Air. Earth. He checked his watch: 3:05 p.m. Had he been wrong? Maybe he'd misread the situation. It wouldn't be the first time. But he *knew* he'd seen her smile.

Wade turned to glance down the block to the right. And then . . .

"Oh my gosh!" His eyes lit up. There she was! Her fire was unmistakable, glowing in the afternoon light as she hurried up to the theater. Wade's vision grew misty with tears of relief, but he pulled it together just as Ember reached him.

"Hi!" he said, waving with awkward enthusiasm.

"Hi," Ember said, more reserved. But there was that beautiful smile of hers. "Sorry I'm late. I had to wait until delivery time to leave."

"That's okay!" Wade couldn't help feeling giddy. "Should . . . should we go in?"

Ember nodded. "Lead the way."

The theater was dimmed by the time they took their seats. Wade noticed other moviegoers scowling because Ember's fire shone brightly in the darkness.

Ember sank down in her seat beside him, embarrassed, pulling her hoodie up over her head. Wade shot the other patrons a chastising look. Could they *be* any ruder? Ember just wanted to watch the movie like any of them!

He sank low in his seat, too, holding out his bucket of popcorn. Ember smiled appreciatively at him before reaching her hand in.

Pop! Pop! Pop! Several of the unpopped kernels at the bottom of the bucket burst when her fire touched them. One even flew out of the bucket and landed in a bald Water guy's head in front of them!

Plunk!

The guy didn't notice as it sank a little, floating in the back of his head.

Wade looked at Ember, his eyes wide.

Ember looked at him, her mouth in the shape of a little squiggle.

Then they both burst into quiet giggles that lasted the entire movie.

"I'm just saying if Mr. Marshy had kept his tide to himself, the movie would have been done in three minutes," Ember insisted as they exited the theater.

"But that's the whole point!" Wade gushed. "The tide ebbs and flows. You can't stop it!"

"Oh, *I* could have," Ember retorted. "Like my dad says, nothing wat—" She stopped herself short. "Uh, I mean, nothing stops Fire."

Ember hoped Wade hadn't caught what she had been about to say. She didn't want to hurt his feelings. It wasn't a very nice expression to begin with.

Luckily, Wade hadn't seemed to notice.

"Ooh, ooh! A photo booth!" Wade rushed forward to a photo booth stationed on the sidewalk. "Let's take a picture!"

"Um, okay." Ember hopped into the booth alongside Wade, careful not to let her fire get too close to him. This really was crazy, being out with a Water guy. Ember knew full well that their elements didn't mix. They couldn't even hold hands—her fire might evaporate him! Or he could extinguish her! But Wade didn't seem to mind her warmth. In fact, he moved closer as they positioned their faces in the frame, his water inevitably bubbling a little. Ember noticed the coolness of his cheek.

"You . . . you smell nice," Ember said.

"Really?" Wade gushed happily. "I'm wearing a new cologne! Acqua di Rio. The salesperson told me it would bring out my inner essence!"

"Inner essence?" Ember raised an eyebrow. "Is that a thing?"

"I don't know." Wade shrugged. "But if you think it smells nice, I'm buying a whole gallon!"

Ember's cheeks glowed pink.

"Oh! The counter's flashing down!" Wade warned her. "Here we go—smile!"

Several snapshots later, the machine printed out two strips of photos with all the funny faces they had made. Except Ember's fire had completely blown out the exposure, and all that was visible were two sets of eyeballs.

"Sorry," Ember said. "I guess the photo booth wasn't made for Fire."

"They're perfect." Wade admired the pictures weepily. "Our first photos!"

He handed Ember her own strip, and she gingerly grasped the edge so she wouldn't burn the memento. It was a little cheesy, but then again, Ember had never taken a photo with anyone except her parents. So in a way, this really was a first for her.

Just then, a clock tower chimed the hour. Ember looked up at the lowering sun. "I should get back before my àshfá wonders where I am."

"Want to meet again tomorrow?" Wade asked hopefully. "I know a café with the best bubble tea you've ever tasted."

"I've never had bubble tea," Ember admitted.

Wade grinned. "Then it's a date!"

Chapter 18

"Wade, where are we going?" Ember raced to keep up with him down a garden pathway on the far side of the city. "I have to be back before the afternoon rush today, or my dad will notice."

"We won't be long!" Wade picked up the pace. "But you've just *gotta* check this out."

"That's what you said yesterday," Ember said, laughing. "And the day before that. And the day before that."

"And I was right, wasn't I?" Wade insisted.

Ember couldn't disagree. The past four days had, in fact, been pretty awesome.

With the culvert doors safely blocked by sandbags, the water leaks in the Fireplace had slowed to a residual trickle. Plus, Wade had sent a message to his old construction crew. He was confident they'd be out to fix the doors by Friday morning at the latest. So all in all, everything was looking up!

"See?" Ember had kissed her àshfá's cheek a couple of days earlier before hurrying out the door to meet Wade in secret. "I told you I had a feeling this water problem would go away."

The receding water had meant business was back to normal in the shop, and Ember had been able to spend the hours she normally had to herself visiting Wade. Though she didn't even want to think about what her àshfá would say if he knew she was hanging out with a Water guy, they had been some of the happiest hours of Ember's life.

She had never realized just how many exciting things there were to do in Element City—even for Fire people! The cafés. The shops. The sights. Wade had taken her to the observation deck of the glass skyscraper she'd imagined climbing as a little spark years earlier. The view from the top had been breathtaking, with sunlight streaming down through the crystal-clear glass ceiling like effervescent gold.

Ember had always assumed that downtown Element City was an unfriendly place for Fire people. But strangely, the more time she spent with Wade, the more comfortable she felt everywhere they went. Some people still stopped and stared. But a lot of folks were friendly. Ember began to wonder if she had been wrong about the city all this time.

"Here it is!" Wade exclaimed as they rounded a bend into a sandy clearing. "What do you think?"

Ember gasped. Stretched before them was a wide lake surrounded by colorful crystal fragments.

"Is this . . . Mineral Lake?" she asked.

"How'd you know?" Wade asked, surprised.

"My dad told me about it." Ember stepped lightly across the sand. "I think he came here once when I was just a baby. Before they'd even started fixing up the shop."

Ember stepped on a pale green crystal, her flame flaring with a matching chartreuse glow.

"Whoa!" Wade exclaimed. "How'd you do that?"

"It's the minerals," she explained. Wade always seemed so impressed by the simple little things she was able to do. Like he was amazed by her just being herself. "Check this out."

Ember ran along the shoreline, skipping from crystal to crystal. Her fire burned with all the colors of the rainbow.

"Awesome!" Wade clapped. "Now watch this!"

With a burst of speed, Wade sprinted out onto the surface of the lake and skidded across, sending up a fine mist of water that refracted the midday sun. Visible for just a moment was a perfect rainbow, arcing through the air.

"It's beautiful." Ember beamed, admiring the picturesque

haven she never would have visited had it not been for Wade. "It's perfect."

"Will I see you again tomorrow?" Wade walked Ember back to the train station.

Ember shook her head. "I'm on register duty Wednesday. I'm not sure I can get away."

A wave of disappointment washed over Wade. He didn't want the magic of this week to end.

"But . . ." Ember added slowly, giving him a dewdrop of hope. "After the culvert doors are fixed, maybe we should celebrate? I mean, you get to keep your job, I get to keep my job, my family gets to keep the shop. That seems worth celebrating, right?"

Wade smiled adoringly at Ember. He wanted so badly to hold her hand. To tell her about the joy he felt every time he saw her perfect, glowing light walking toward him. Wade couldn't explain it, but just knowing Ember made him feel like he had a purpose. He wanted to be there for her, to help her burn the brightest she could. He had been adrift for so long. It was nice feeling like he finally had a direction.

"You bet," Wade said. "We should definitely celebrate."

Chapter 19

Ember couldn't stop grinning as she sketched in her notebook. The lunchtime rush had settled down in the Fireplace, and she had a few minutes to herself by the register. Quiet moments like these were her favorite time to doodle new sign ideas for the Fireplace. But her happy glow wasn't because of the picture on the paper before her.

Carefully, she snuck a peek under her notebook at the blown-out photo strip of her and Wade from earlier that week. Even though only their eyes were visible, Ember loved the way Wade's eyes seemed to sparkle in the picture.

"Ember?" Her mother's voice came from behind her.

Ember whirled, startled. She quickly covered the photo strip with her notebook.

"Hey—hi! I mean, what's up, Àshká?" Ember awkwardly leaned an elbow on her notebook.

Cinder gave her a quizzical look. "A customer up front needs help making a gemstone selection." She sniffed the air a little—and smiled. "And . . . I have a couple waiting for a smoke reading in the back. Could you please help the customer up front?"

"Oh, sure thing!" Ember hopped out from behind the register. *That* had been close. She didn't want anyone catching her looking at the photo strip. Her àshká's seeing it would cause curiosity. Curiosity would lead to questions. And questions would lead to *assumptions*. All over a picture of eyeballs—let alone if her àshká found out who those eyeballs belonged to!

Still, nothing could snuff out Ember's cheerful mood. She hummed a little tune she and Wade had heard at a café as she approached the customer.

"*Rái khìf!*" she greeted the customer. "How can I help?"

The customer turned. She was a middle-aged Fire woman wearing loose flowing robes and many bangles. "Ah, yes!" she said in a tinkly voice. "I need help choosing the right bauble."

"Sure!" Ember said. "I can help with that. What did you have in mind?"

"I want something *mystical*." The woman's eyes looked huge behind her oversized glasses. "Do you have something like that?"

"Ummm." Ember checked out the gemstone necklaces on display. "This sun-shaped one is very pretty. It has a sparkly, mystical vibe to it."

The robed customer frowned. "No, no. That's not quite right. I'm thinking something more . . . otherworldly."

"Oh." Ember reconsidered all the gemstones. There were twinkling yellow citrine bracelets from the Sand Isles and deep onyx pendants from the Kol Islands. They all looked pretty as they caught the light. But in truth, Ember didn't have a clue what an "otherworldly" gemstone might look like.

"How about this one?" She pulled down a particularly deep ruby necklace that burned crimson in her fire. "This one has an otherworldly feel to it, I think."

The customer squinted behind her huge glasses. "Hmmmm. Is this your first time helping a customer?"

"Uh . . ." Ember felt a familiar flicker of anger ignite inside her. "No, actually, I've been helping customers since the Fireplace first opened. I'm going to run the store—one day."

"Really?" The customer eyed her. "But your aura shines so . . . inexperienced."

Flames roiled in Ember's chest. With an effort, she forced them back down and gave a tight laugh. "Heh."

The customer turned her attention back to the trinkets. "No, what I had in mind was something to bring out my . . . *inner essence.*"

At those words, an image of Wade's smiling face flashed through Ember's mind. She pictured his goofy enthusiasm beside her in the photo booth. *If you like it, I'll buy a whole gallon!* he had gushed about the cologne that brought out his "inner essence." Ember stifled a giggle, and a cool wave of calm rushed over her. The idea of an inner essence was so ridiculous. But if that's what this customer wanted, maybe she could channel her "inner Wade" to help pick the right bauble.

"Oh!" Ember said enthusiastically. "I think I understand. What you want . . ." She reached up and selected a gemstone necklace of soft pink that matched the embroidered blossoms running along the woman's robes. Taking a pinch of sand from a nearby display, Ember delicately formed a swirl of glass waves around the gem. "Is something original, to match your soul."

"Ooooh!" The customer's eyes lit up. "*Yes!* This is perfect! An original! Oh, Ashley *will* be jealous!" She took the necklace eagerly and, without so much as a thank-you, hurried to a mirror to try it on.

Ember smiled and shook her head. Some people's "inner essence" was truly something.

"Ember?"

138

For the second time, Ember was startled. She turned to find her àshfá standing behind her, carrying a crate of new inventory.

"You helped the customer?" he asked.

"Oh, yeah." Ember nodded. "She wanted a gemstone. I helped her pick one."

"Mmm." Her àshfá watched as the customer posed before the mirror. "She seems like . . . a tricky customer."

"Hah." Ember laughed. "She's original, that's for sure."

Bernie nodded, his eyes on his daughter now. He seemed impressed.

"Good daughter," he said. "Help me unload the new inventory."

"Sure thing!" Ember agreed. "Let me just grab my notebook with the supply list."

She hurried to the register, but when she got there, she gasped. She'd left the corner of the photo strip peeking out from underneath!

"Flame!" she whispered. "I could have sworn I covered that."

Quickly, she grabbed the notebook and tucked the photo strip into her pocket. She was *definitely* not ready to tell her parents about Wade yet.

Probably ever.

Chapter 20

"She's *incredible*, Mom!"

Wade gushed to his family in the middle of their living room pool. His mom, Brook, and brother, Alan, sat on inflatable armchairs while Wade was pooled up in the middle of the water like a bubbling fountain of happiness. Meanwhile, his younger sibling, Lake, video-conferenced in from art school on a laptop that floated on a nearby raft.

"I've never met someone like her!" Wade could barely take a breath because he was bawling so many tears of joy. "She's fiery and tender and driven and smart and oh my gosh, Mom, she's *so* creative! You should see the stuff she's able to make, like hot-air balloons out of scrap metal, and she turned all different colors down by the lake. And gosh, I want to hold her hand but I'm not sure if she wants me to because every time I get close, she acts like she's afraid she'll evaporate me. I'm worried I'll put out her fire, but I really, really, really, really want to hold her hand!"

"Oh, I'm so happy for my baby boy!" Brook dabbed the corner of her eye with a handkerchief. "He's found his soulmate. The ebb to his flow."

"Just remember to play it cool, buddy," Alan advised, though his eyes, too, were misty. "Girls like mystery. Show her your emotions are a deep ocean of intrigue. Play hard to get."

"Excuse me?" Alan's wife, Eddy, called out from the other room, where she was wrangling their sons, Marco and Polo, as they tried to jump on the waterbed. "Wade—do *not* listen to your brother. He doesn't know what he's talking about. The only thing that's going to be hard to get is his way back home if he doesn't come in here and help me control these two little sea monsters!"

Alan sighed. "Be right back."

"Eddy's right." Brook took Wade's hands. "Tell Ember everything. Let your feelings flow."

"It's just . . . Mom, sometimes I'm scared of *how* much I like her." Wade sniffled. "What if she doesn't feel the same way?"

His mom smiled. "There's only one way of knowing."

"Do you want me to paint you a picture?" Lake asked dryly from the computer. "To literally show her your feelings?"

"Really?" Wade asked excitedly. "Could you?"

Lake rolled their eyes. But their half smile seemed to indicate that even cynical Lake was drawn in by his emotion. "Maybe. I'll see what Ghibli and I can whirl up."

Wade bubbled with fresh excitement. "It's just, I've never felt so *happy*. Being with Ember feels right. She's so strong, Mom. She doesn't even know it yet. But together, we could do anything."

"Does that mean you *like* her, Uncle Wade?" Marco popped up from the living room pool and spit out a little fountain of water.

Wade grinned. "You bet, buddy!"

"But do you *like* like her?" Polo asked, popping up beside his brother. "Like, a double like?"

"Sure?" Wade said, getting a little confused.

"Ewwwww!" Marco and Polo shouted together. "Uncle Wade has the double-like cooties! Wash them off! Wash them off!"

The two kids splashed Wade relentlessly, and Wade pretended to growl before creating a giant wave that rushed the rascals across the room.

"Yeah!" they cheered, flowing up and over the living room furniture.

"See what I mean?" Eddy splashed in, disheveled from kid wrangling. "This is what your brother has taught them. Double-like cooties."

"Hey, I double-like you." Alan nudged Eddy's arm.

Eddy made a little exasperated sound but couldn't help smiling. "Me too."

"I think the real question everyone is asking is"—Brook looked deep into Wade's eyes—"how *much* do you like Ember?"

Wade got teary just contemplating it.

"I think . . . I double-like Ember more than I've ever double-liked anyone in my entire life."

Chapter 21

Thursday morning dawned bright, sunlight streaming across Ember's bedroom. Stretching, she breathed deeply as the sun's rays warmed her face, bolstering her fire. Today was going to be a good day. She could feel it.

After a quick breakfast of Char Crisps, Ember cheerfully tied her apron and headed downstairs to begin her register duty. She reached the bottom of the staircase, taking note of the few early-morning customers who were already perusing the shelves.

By the pyramid can display, an elderly man was using his cane to maneuver a can from the very bottom.

"Here, let me help you." Ember hurried over and gently guided his cane away from the bottom can, selecting one from the top of the pile. "Did you need anything else?"

"Chili oil," the man said in a croaky voice.

"Right this way!" Ember led him to an aisle with glass bottles. "The one up there is on sale. It's a very good price for some of the best chili oil from Fire Land. Would you like that one?"

The man studied the bottles. *"Sòbê sh sfá."* He switched to Firish, saying *I'll take that one.*

Ember stood on her tiptoes and pulled down a bottle from the highest shelf. But when she handed it to the customer, she could see from the look on his face that he was displeased with the torn label on the bottle.

"Would you prefer another?" she offered.

The man nodded. *"Ìshkshá." Please.*

Ember smiled kindly and put back the bottle with the torn label before selecting a replacement.

As the man took his basket to the register, Ember noticed her àshfá watching her from where he was making kol nuts. She grinned and gave him a little wave. Her àshfá smiled back, the glow of the morning sun making his face look just a bit younger. Days like this in the shop, Ember thought, were the best. Where everything seemed like the old days, when she was just a little spark. Happy. Bright. This was the way she wanted the shop to feel when, one day, she took over.

Suddenly, a deep rumble echoed through the walls, and Ember's eyes widened as bricks crumbled, revealing a burst pipe leaking water. The spray pooled onto the floor with alarming speed, heading straight for the Blue Flame cauldron!

"No, no, no, no, no!" Ember cried.

"The water is back!" Bernie shouted.

Together, they rushed to save the Blue Flame cauldron from getting doused, scraping it along the tile floor to the side of the shop. Then Ember ran to the pipe and heated the metal, welding the crack sealed again.

Why is the water back? she thought frantically. *It shouldn't be back—we blocked the culvert! Wade's construction friends must almost be done with the repairs by this point. What is going on?*

"Ember Lumen!" A voice at the front of the store suddenly rang out.

Ember and Bernie turned toward the door in tandem, both bewildered. A courier stood there, holding numerous huge vases of flowers.

"Delivery for Ember Lumen," the man called.

"What the—" Ember started. She looked at the gigantic vases in utter confusion. Had Wade sent her flowers? To the *shop*?

That was when she noticed two big watery eyes staring out from one of the vases.

Ember gasped as her mother stepped in to accept the delivery. "Flowers for Ember?"

Panicking, Ember sprinted to beat her mom to the courier.

"Oh, these *are* beautiful!" She grabbed the vases. "I'll just . . . put these away."

Before her parents could ask any questions, Ember rushed to the basement and put the vases on the floor.

"What are you doing here?" she hissed to the two big eyes watching her from one of the vases. Though a part of her was a teensy bit flattered Wade had come to visit her in flowers, this had to be the worst possible place and time!

Before Ember's eyes, Wade popped his head up from the vase. "I've got bad news," he said, pouring the water from the other vases into his and re-forming into his full size. "The sandbags didn't hold."

"Uh, obviously!" Ember said. "The water is back in the pipes."

"And I've also got worse news." Wade dripped with embarrassment. "I'd forgotten a tiny detail about the last time I saw that city crew. See, the reason I got fired from the construction site was because I caused a cement explosion that trapped the guys for . . . a while. I guess you could say they still have *hard feelings*. Hah. Because they won't help us."

"Wade," Ember said gravely, "Gale's deadline is *tomorrow*. We'll need more sandbags."

"But that didn't work before," Wade pointed out.

Ember flared. "Well, I can't do nothing!"

Just then, the basement door burst open. To Ember's horror, her father marched down the staircase.

"Ember, did you fix the leak?" Bernie called. When he laid eyes on Wade, his fire fumed. "It's you again!" he shouted.

Wade looked behind himself, then pointed comically to his own chest. "Who, me?"

"You're the guy who started all this!" Bernie thundered. He grabbed a nearby fire poker and swung at Wade.

"Ahh!" Wade jumped back.

"No, Dad!" Ember rushed to stop him. "Different guy!"

But Bernie spotted the City Inspector badge on Wade's chest. "You are a city inspector?"

"Uh . . ." Wade looked to Ember for help.

She shook her head urgently.

"No. I am not an inspector." Wade covered his badge with his hand. But his water only magnified the word *INSPECTOR*.

"You *are* an inspector!" Bernie shouted. "Why are you poking around? Is this because of the water leak?"

"No!" Ember interjected. "Not because of water in *any* way. He's a different kind of inspector." She shot Wade a meaningful look. "Right?"

"Uh—yeah!" Wade caught on. "I'm a—food inspector! I've come to inspect your food."

Ember smacked her head.

"Hmmmm." Bernie eyed him suspiciously. "Okay. The food is upstairs. Come."

As Bernie led the group back up to the shop, Ember fumed quietly.

"Food inspector?" she hissed at Wade.

"I panicked!" Wade whispered.

Upstairs, Bernie slammed a big bowl of burning kol nuts down on a table in front of Wade. "You're really a food inspector?" he asked smugly. "Then inspect *this*."

"Dad . . ." Ember tried to shut this down.

But her dad waved her silent.

Customers had gathered when they heard the commotion around the counter where Wade was presented with the spicy Fire Land specialty. Everyone watched intently, holding their collective breath as Wade tentatively spooned up a white-hot glowing kol nut.

With a nervous laugh, he looked to Ember before gingerly placing the kol nut in his mouth and swallowing. Everyone gasped.

Wade grimaced. The kol nut sizzled all the way down. Slowly, he gave Ember a pained smile, perhaps thinking the worst was over.

He was mistaken.

"FIRE!" Wade screamed as the true heat from the kol nut hit

him. He clamped a hand over his mouth. But the pain and surprise grew inside him, forming a huge scream bubble that wriggled its way up and out of his mouth through his hand.

"AHHH!" Wade released the scream as the bubble popped.

Finally, the heat passed, and Wade simmered down, coughing, before giving a weak thumbs-up.

"See?" Ember told her àshfá hurriedly. "He likes it! Now he can go."

"Hmmm." Bernie grunted, still not satisfied. "Did we pass?"

"Mmm-hmm," Wade croaked hoarsely. "A-plus."

A moment later, Wade started licking his lips. "Actually," he said thoughtfully, "after the heat dies down, that tastes really good."

Ember watched with growing dread as Wade scooped a kol nut into a mug and dripped some water on it to snuff out the flame. She frantically motioned to Wade to stop what he was doing. But it was no use. He gulped the cooled kol nut down in one go.

"It's really tasty if you water it down a little." Wade grinned at Bernie, presumably thinking he was offering a compliment.

But Bernie flared hotter than any kol nut in Fire Land.

"Water us down?" he screamed. "WATER US DOWN?!"

In a fury, Bernie whipped out a camera from the register drawer and snapped Wade's picture.

"We will *never* be watered down by you! GET OUT!"

As quickly as she could, Ember rushed Wade out the door. "All right, sir. You've got to go," she said in as authoritative of a tone as she could muster, given the shock coursing through her body.

Outside, Ember didn't even know what to think. "That's the most upset I've ever seen my dad," she said shakily. "Look, meet me at the beach and we'll make more sandbags." What else could they do at this point? They were out of options.

Ember glanced back at the door, then at Wade. He seemed to understand. She had to go back inside, and he just had to go.

Wade sprinted off down the sidewalk.

As Ember slowly headed back into the store, she realized with a pang that her àshfá was pinning Wade's photograph to the bulletin board behind the register. Wade's terrified expression stared out from the photo, and the photo was seared across the top with the word *BANNED*.

Bernie continued ranting about Wade until he broke into a massive coughing fit and collapsed to the floor, his flame smoking out a little.

"Dad!" Ember and her mother rushed to his side. Gently, Ember lifted him up, feeding him a stick to build back his flame.

"Àshfá, it's going to be okay," she comforted him. "It's all going to be okay."

She snuck a worried glance at Wade's picture. Everything that had just happened was a humongous mess. The water was back. They weren't sure how to fix it. And now Wade was banned from the shop.

How much worse would the reaction be if her àshfá ever found out she and Wade were friends?

Chapter 22

The sun was setting in the distance as Ember furiously shoveled sand into bags that Wade held open for her. They had met at the beach near the broken culvert doors. To their dismay, their suspicions had been correct—the sandbags from earlier that week had given way, and water was continuing to spill through from the main canal.

Ember dug and dug, beads of lava sweat rolling down her temple. They *had* to get those culvert doors closed again. And she was going to do it even if she had to dig down to the center of the planet.

Wade, however, looked doubtful. "I don't think this is going to work."

"Well, it won't if you don't hold the bag straight." Ember gritted her teeth and dug harder.

"Maybe your dad will understand," Wade insisted.

Ember scoffed, a burning ball of frustration simmering painfully inside her. She heaved a massive mound of sand into the bag.

"I'm serious," Wade pressed. "Look, I know it can be tough. I mean, with my dad, we were like oil and water." He paused. "I never got the chance to fix that. But you guys are different. It might be time to tell him."

Ember couldn't believe what she was hearing. Wade didn't have *any* idea what he was talking about. His dad was nothing like her àshfá. His dad hadn't given up his whole family—his whole *life*—for—for—

"Yeah, right," she snapped more accusingly than she'd intended. "And say what? That I got us shut down AND DESTROYED HIS DREAM?"

Saddened, frustrated, empty, Ember sank down to her knees, her flame slowly burning down to a gentle flicker. Wade's nervous expression made her feel wretched. It wasn't his fault; he was trying to help. None of this was his fault. It was hers. All hers.

"I think I'm failing," she said miserably. "My àshfá should have retired *years* ago, but he doesn't think I'm ready." Ember's chest rose and fell with overwhelming sadness. "You have no idea how hard they've worked or what they've had to endure—the family they left behind. How do you repay a sacrifice that big?" The words she dreaded admitting burned her throat. "It . . . it all feels like a burden. But how can I say that? I'm a bad daughter."

Ember didn't expect Wade to come near her again, especially after her outburst. But she suddenly felt the familiar coolness of his arm next to hers.

"Hey, no," he comforted her. "You're doing your best."

Ember couldn't help scoffing a little. Wade's sentiment was sweet, but he didn't get it. No one cared if she was doing her best if all her best did was mess everything up. She suddenly realized her flame was so low that her inner light was fully exposed, casting prismatic colors around her. For Ember, it was humiliating. She hadn't meant to be so fragile and vulnerable.

"I'm a mess," she sniffed, attempting to bolster her flame back up.

But before she could, Wade shook his head. "Nah. I think you're even more beautiful."

Ember realized Wade was smiling at her with those adoring eyes of his. And despite her sadness, she smiled a little, too.

"Maybe you're right when you said my temper was trying to tell me something," she admitted.

Ember and Wade gazed into each other's eyes for a long moment, the brilliant blue of his irises reflecting her flame like sparkles. Wade scooted closer—perhaps closer than they had ever dared be to each other.

Suddenly, he noticed the glass beneath Ember. "Whoa." He breathed. "Look what your fire did to the sand. It's glass."

Ember looked down at the smooth surface. Without really thinking, she scooped up a shard of the glass, melting it in her hands and forming it into a perfectly round sphere. She used delicate tendrils of fire to etch a design inside.

"Wow." Wade breathed. "It looks like a Vivisteria flower."

Ember nodded sadly. When she was a teenager, she used to sketch the flower over and over in her notebooks. Now here she was as an adult etching the blossom she knew she would never touch into something even more finite. Fragility trapped within the repercussions of her temper. Beauty sealed behind glass.

Sealed behind glass . . .

Ember's eyes suddenly glowed wide, and she gazed at the culvert. "I know how to seal those doors."

Wade stood back while Ember approached the piles of sandbags stacked up against the culvert doors and watched as she took a deep, deep breath, placing her hands against them.

What happened next sent ripples of emotion coursing through him, as though he were watching a master artist at work.

In a brilliant white flash, Ember flared, her fire consuming the entire sand pile. But the glow and heat were different from before. Rather than violent, this explosion was—controlled. Massively powerful as it spread across every single granule. Wade stood mesmerized. It reminded him of standing beside his father as a young boy, screaming his feelings out into the ocean, except instead of waiting for the emotion to dissipate out over the waves, Ember's fire was directed, smoothing the sand with a purpose. He'd never imagined anything like this was possible.

With a final surge, Ember melted the entire sandpile into solid waves of glass several feet thick, completely sealing the culvert doors.

Wade couldn't describe what he was feeling as Ember returned to his side. The magnitude of what he'd just witnessed—the honor of just being in the presence of such a powerful Element. The tears began flowing. He couldn't stop them.

"Again with the crying?" Ember asked, though her expression defied the sarcasm. She was impressed with her own efforts, too.

"It's . . . just . . ." Wade blubbered. "I've never been punched in the face with beauty before!"

Without warning, the ground beneath them rumbled. A massive ship was passing by in the main canal.

"Moment of truth," Ember said quietly beside him.

Together, they watched as the ship rolled past, a titanic wall of water plunging over the spillover ledge in its wake. The deluge rushed up against the glass seal on the door, rising higher and higher . . . and then, it settled. The water began draining as intended into the spillover. Not a drop passed by the sealed doors.

"It worked!" Ember exclaimed.

Without thinking, Wade reached out to embrace her, to dance with joyful celebration in the moonlight.

But before he could touch her, Ember drew back, breaking the moment. A little sheepishly, Wade brought his arms to his side. Still, they had done it! Ember had done it. If only she could see what he saw—that she was the strongest Element he had ever known.

"I'll have Gale come by right after work," Wade promised. "I'll let you know the second I hear anything."

"Do you think this will be good enough for her?" Ember asked.

Wade looked at the wall of glass. Boy, he hoped it was. "It's hard to know. She could go either way."

The worry on Ember's face was tangible. Wade desperately wanted to hold her and tell her everything was going to be okay.

Instead, he pulled out the glass Vivisteria sphere she had made earlier.

"I saved this for you." He handed it to Ember, and the beautiful keepsake glimmered in her light. "It's special."

Chapter 23

Friday evening, Ember lay in bed, turning the Vivisteria flower sphere over and over in her hands. The whole day had gone by, and there was still no word from Wade. It was too risky for him to come to the Fireplace anymore, and even talking on the phone might rouse her parents' suspicions. They had agreed he would send her a signal of some kind once he had an update. He'd even given her his address in the Water District in case of an emergency. Ember had anxiously watched the door of the shop all day for a sign—any sign—from Wade that the news from Gale was good. But as the sun started to set and the shop sign switched to CLOSED, she began to worry—what if the news was bad and Wade didn't have the heart to tell her?

"He'll come through," Ember reassured herself. "He wouldn't let me down like that."

The Vivisteria sphere twinkled in her firelight. It was funny—she had made it, and yet she almost couldn't believe it. The flower etched inside was so . . . perfect. How had she done that?

A cough echoed downstairs, and Ember stopped turning the sphere to listen. Her àshfá was still in the shop.

Quietly, she tiptoed downstairs. Her father was by the brick wall, repairing the crumbled patch from the day before. He looked tired in the ethereal glow of the Blue Flame.

"Àshfá?" Ember asked. "You okay?"

Her father turned and gave her a weary smile. "Yes, yes. Just too much to fix."

Ember pulled over a stool and sat beside him. "I'll take care of it. *You* need to rest."

"Yes, ma'am!" Bernie replied. They laughed, and Bernie took Ember's hands.

"Ember, I see a change in you," he said. "Happier. Calmer with customers and with that . . . food inspector. Always putting the shop first. You have proven I can trust you."

Ember stared down at her àshfá's hands. She felt guilty. None of this would have even happened if it hadn't been for her. The risk to the shop—her father's dream—was squarely her responsibility. She didn't deserve her father's trust. But she didn't have the courage to tell him why.

Bernie coughed again, and before he could hide it, the flame in his hand flickered.

"Àshfá?" Ember asked, concerned.

He just shook his head. "I'm so lucky I have you."

Bernie patted her cheek. Then, wearily, he trudged up the stairs, leaving Ember alone in the silent glow of the Blue Flame cauldron.

She watched him go, fear creeping in. If the worst happened . . . if the store *was* shut down . . . Ember wasn't certain her father could recover from a blow that hard.

There was no choice—she simply couldn't wait any longer. She *had* to know if Gale was going to cancel the citations.

Ember glanced at Wade's picture on the BANNED wall. It was silly, but she longed for his coolness next to her and the reassuring hope in his eyes.

Right now, the only person she needed was Wade.

She pulled out the tiny piece of paper with his address on it. And, coming to a decision, she silently left through the shop door, strapped on her scooter helmet, and drove out into the night.

Chapter 24

"Ember! You found it!" Wade's eyes welled up with fresh emotion. Ember Lumen was standing on his doorstep in the Water District! He noticed her expression. "Everything okay?"

"Please tell me that you have some good news from Gale." Ember removed her scooter helmet, her face oddly drawn. "I'm getting really worried about my dad. This has to break my way."

Wade wished he could give Ember the news she wanted. "I haven't heard from her yet, but she *swore* she'd call tonight." Suddenly Wade had a thought bubble. "Actually, my family stopped by for dinner. Do you want to come up and wait for the call together?"

"Your family?" Ember seemed uncertain.

Wade nodded, internally praying, *Please say yes. Please say yes!*

"Okay," Ember finally agreed. "I'll come up for a bit."

Yes! Wade gave himself a mental high five. Beaming from ear to ear, he escorted Ember into the lobby of the sleek and sophisticated Progress Towers.

Ember looked taken aback by the spaciousness of the atrium and the serene waterfalls that cascaded along every surface.

"I'm sorry . . . you *live* here?"

Wade rubbed the back of his neck. He wanted to say, *Yup! This baby is all mine!* But he couldn't. Because that would be lying. "It's my mom's place," he admitted.

He led Ember to a crystal-clear elevator that would zip them up twenty stories to his mom's apartment. He loved watching Ember marvel at the interior architecture. Every surface of the Progress Towers was made from either water or glass, which meant that Ember's beautiful shining light reflected off everything. Even the moisture in the air gathered around her in a fine mist as though she were a fiery angel.

On the twentieth floor, Wade led Ember down the hall to his mom's apartment. Brook opened the door and beamed when she saw Ember standing beside her son.

"Ember! I'm so excited to finally meet you!" Instinctively, she reached out to hug Ember—the Ripple family was a family of huggers, after all—but Wade urgently shook his head. Brook got the message.

"Oh, uh, do we hug?" Brook asked uncertainly. "Or wave? I don't want to put you out—ha ha."

"Um, a hello is fine," Ember said.

"Hardly." Brook winked at Ember. "Wade hasn't stopped talking about you since the day you met. The boy is smitten!"

"Mom!" Wade complained.

"Oh, come on!" Brook waved them into the apartment. "I'm your mother. I know when something's lighting you up. I just didn't know she would be so *smoky*."

They laughed. But Wade could tell Ember was uncomfortable.

"Come this way!" Brook insisted. "Meet the rest of the family."

As they stepped inside, Wade leaned down to whisper to Ember. "Hey, you okay?"

"Yeah," Ember said quietly. "Just, uh, make sure I don't get put out? Or, you know, say anything too smoky?"

Wade smiled. "Don't worry. They're going to love you."

Ember didn't want to burst Wade's bubble, but everything inside his mom's apartment was basically a death trap for Fire.

There were waterfalls and water features and waterworks. For Flame's sake, the entire living room was one giant pool with inflatable furniture. It was like that old children's game "the floor is lava," except in that game, Fire children wanted to step in the lava. In this situation, Ember wasn't sure she could step anywhere.

She lingered back hesitantly until Wade came to the rescue, grabbing the welcome mat from the front door and tossing it over an inflatable raft so Ember could climb on. Precariously, she balanced on the one piece of furniture that would *not* snuff her out, and Wade guided her to the dining area to meet the rest of his family.

"Hi!" Alan waved. "We've got two kids swimming around here somewhere. Marco! Polo!"

Without warning, two little Water heads popped up out of the pool beside Ember's raft. "Hi, Uncle Wade!" they shouted. Their eyes grew large when they saw Ember.

"Do you *die* if you fall in water?" Marco asked, dead serious. He shook the raft a little for good measure.

"Whoa!" Ember put her arms out, unstable.

"Marco!" Wade shouted.

Alan pulled Marco away from the raft. "Easy there, kiddo!" He turned to Ember with an apologetic expression. "Kids. Heh, heh. Please don't hate us."

"Anyway . . ." Wade pushed Ember's raft along toward the dining table. "That's my little sib, Lake, and their girlfriend, Ghibli. They're students at Element City School for the Arts."

"Sup," greeted Ghibli.

"Following in Mom's wake," Lake added.

"Oh, nonsense." Brook swept out carrying a platter of Water food for dinner. "I'm just an architect. The real artist is my brother Harold."

Off to the side, a shorter Water man Ember hadn't noticed until then was standing beside a large painting. "Oh, I just dabble in watercolors," Harold said humbly. "Or, as we like to call them, *colors*."

The entire Ripple family broke into laughter.

Meanwhile, Ember took it all in from her personal little Fire island. Wade's family was huge. What was it like growing up with so many . . . people? Ember's world had always been so concise: just her mom and her dad and their shop. She didn't want to be unsociable. But it all felt overwhelming.

Brook finished setting the table and motioned everyone over. "Oh, don't listen to Harold," she told Ember. "He's a wonderful painter. One of his paintings just got into the Element City Museum's permanent collection."

"Wow." Ember tried to join the flow of conversation. "That is so cool. My only talent is 'Clean up on aisle four!'"

"Talk about being modest!" Wade took a seat next to Ember, gazing at her adoringly. "Ember's got an incredible creative flame. I've never seen anything like it!"

"I just have to say," Harold jumped in, speaking very deliberately, "you speak *so* well and clear."

It took Ember a moment to understand what he was talking about. Then it dawned on her: Harold must have been assuming that Firish was her native language—that she hadn't been born in Element City.

Wade shot his uncle a look, but Ember kept her cool.

"Yeah," she said, deflecting the awkward moment, "it's amazing what talking in the same language your whole life can do."

"Gah!" Harold's cheeks flushed pink with embarrassment.

Alan quickly changed the topic. "Hey, Ember, did Wade ever tell you that he's deathly afraid of sponges?"

"No," Ember said, intrigued.

"I was traumatized." Wade's eyes grew distant. He recounted his fateful encounter with a sponge at school years earlier.

When he finished, everyone started cracking up—Ember included. She watched everyone laughing together, passing around the food. She had a sudden flashback to dinner with her parents. Warm, cozy, but subdued. Was this what a family dinner was supposed to be like?

Could this be what her àshfá had left behind?

Just then, Alan reached for a pitcher, but the glass handle slipped from his fingers and the pitcher shattered on the table.

"Alan, that was new!" Brook groaned.

"Oh, I can fix it," Ember offered. Deftly, she picked up the broken shards and melted them together. The warmth of the molten glass in her hands felt comfortingly familiar. Enjoying the sensation of being in her element, she re-formed the glowing mass into a new pitcher with a graceful curved handle and etched flowers blossoming up the side. When she was finished, she admired it.

It took her a moment to realize everyone was staring at her.

"Oh, um, sorry." She quickly placed the pitcher on the table, embarrassed.

"That . . . was . . . incredible." Harold looked like he'd just witnessed a miracle.

The entire family applauded, and Ember flushed with appreciation. No one had ever applauded her for anything before. "It's just melted glass."

"Just melted glass?" Brook looked at her incredulously. "Every building in the new city is built from 'just melted glass.' Oh, no. You *have* to do something with that talent!"

Ember's fire flushed an even deeper red. Talent? Was she truly talented?

"See?" Wade leaned in close, his cheek a whisper of cool mist. "I told you you're special."

Chapter 25

Finishing dinner at the Ripple household meant only one thing: a round of the Crying Game. Wade couldn't wait to show Ember how to play! He excitedly positioned her raft alongside the rest of his family as he assigned teams.

"Okay. It's me, Mom, Lake, and Eddy versus Alan, Harold, Ghibli, and Ember. Here's how the rules work."

Ember interrupted him. "Let me guess. You have to cry?"

Wade wagged his finger. "We try *not* to cry."

Ember raised an eyebrow at him, and Wade felt his stomach turn to puddles all over again. Everything about this was so perfect. Ember was fitting in *great* with his folks!

Brook picked up a tiny hourglass and nodded to her opponent, Harold.

"You have one minute to make Mom cry," Wade told him. "Go!"

Brook flipped the hourglass.

Harold held her gaze intently.

"Nineteen seventy-nine. November. You were—"

Brook instantly burst into sobs.

"Awww!" groaned Wade, Lake, and Eddy while the opposing team splashed high fives, except for Ember, who mimed an air high five from a safe distance.

"I never got a chance to say goodbye to Nana!" Brook bawled. "You're good, Harold!"

Harold folded his arms, pleased with himself. "Okay. Ember, Wade, you're up."

"Yeah, this is almost unfair," Ember said as Wade moved her raft to the middle of the room. "Because I have literally never cried. You got no chance."

"Sounds like a challenge," Wade retorted.

Harold flipped the timer. "Go!"

Wade looked Ember dead in the eye. "Butterfly," he said dramatically. "Windshield wipers. Half a butterfly."

Around him, his whole family started sniffling. But Ember didn't even flinch.

"Okay." Wade racked his brain for a story that might tug at Ember's heartstrings. Oh! He had a good one! "An old man on his deathbed," Wade began. "He remembers the summer he fell in love.

She was out of his league, and he was young and scared." Wade's lower lip quivered. "He let her go, thinking surely summer would come again. It never did."

The entire family burst into tears. But Ember remained unmoved. She crossed her arms and just smiled confidently.

"Almost out of time," Harold warned.

The story of the old man had always gotten to Wade, but something about it was different this time—the idea of grieving for his lost love, knowing that everything could have been different if he'd had the courage to share his feelings. It rang truer now than ever. And it was more than Wade could bear.

"Ember," Wade said, his voice suddenly serious. "When I met you, I thought I was drowning. But that light—that light inside you has made me feel so alive. And all I want now is to be near it. Near you. Together."

As he spoke, Ember's expression changed. The bravado fell away, and they locked eyes, her gaze all at once vulnerable and uncertain. Wade couldn't exactly read her expression. Her glow burned warm, but her eyes looked anxious. Something was holding her back.

A lone lava tear beaded up in the corner of Ember's eye. It slowly trickled down her cheek and landed in the water pool with a sizzle.

Around them, the family sat stunned.

Then the phone rang.

Wade and Ember snapped toward the sound, the connection broken.

Coming back to himself, Wade gasped. "It's Gale."

He scrambled to pick up the phone, sloshing as he went. "Hello? Gale?"

His boss's stormy voice echoed on the other end. "*Glass?* You repaired it with *glass*?"

Wade's stomach plummeted. Ember's eyes were on him, aching for good news. But, splash buckets, this didn't sound good.

Just then, there was muffled commotion on the other end of the line.

"Hold the storm," Gale said.

Wade heard a few thumping noises in the background, like something heavy was being banged against a window.

"You used *tempered* glass?" Gale's voice came back on the line.

"Uh . . . yeah?" Wade said. Ember's eyes were practically burning into him, she was so anxious.

"Huh." Gale sounded impressed. "I would never have thought of that. Don't know how you kids did it. But it's solid as a rock. That Fire girlfriend of yours must have used some serious heat to make this stuff. I like it." There was a pause. "Consider the citations canceled."

Wade broke into a grin and beamed at Ember. The hope that flooded her eyes was beyond beautiful.

"We did it?" she asked.

"We did it!" Wade cheered.

The entire family burst into a whirlpool of celebration. Ember sank down onto her doormat raft, looking like she might melt with relief.

Wade gazed at her, his vision blurred with joyful tears.

Nothing meant more to him in that moment than that she was okay.

"Thank you, Mrs. Ripple," Ember said as she left Brook's apartment. "This was really great."

If Ember could have reached out and hugged every single member of the Ripple family, she would have. She was just . . . so relieved. They had done it. She and Wade had done it! Her àshfá's shop was safe. It wasn't going to get shut down—his dream would stay alive. Ember had never been through so much turmoil in her entire life. After a week like this, she seriously couldn't wait for things to go back to normal.

"It was wonderful to finally meet you." Wade's mom smiled kindly at Ember. "And I meant what I said about your talent. I have a friend who runs the best glassmaking firm in the world. During dinner, I slipped out and I made a call. And I told her about you. They're looking for an intern. It could be an amazing opportunity."

A sudden spark lit in Ember's chest. Glassmaking? Her talent? An internship? "For real?" she asked, not fully processing what Wade's mom was saying.

Brook nodded. "It's a long way from the city, but it would be an incredible start." She held up the pitcher Ember had made. "Look at me! I have an original Ember!"

Ember looked at the pitcher. Every masterful etch of glass refracted the light just right. It was a small piece of perfection that she—Ember—had made . . . and it was something that had the potential to take her away from everything and everyone she had ever known.

"I—" Ember started. She had never considered anything like this. A job that wasn't at the shop? That wasn't even in Element City? Glassmaking? Art? No, she couldn't. Could she? Should she? Her thoughts all collided at once. What was happening?

"Hold up. I'll walk you out." Wade bounded over, still looking elated after the good news from Gale.

Ember waved goodbye awkwardly to his mom, and Brook

shut the door. Ember numbly stepped into the elevator along-side Wade.

A job outside Element City? Leave home? Her parents? She would never do that. She *couldn't* do that. After everything they had sacrificed for her, leaving home was unthinkable. Out of the question. The shop was her future. It was her father's dream. It was everything she'd worked toward her entire life.

So why, for the second time that day, did she feel like crying?

Chapter 26

Out. Ember had to get out. She had to get back home where she belonged.

"Whoa, Ember! Hold up!" Wade's voice echoed behind her in the atrium. But Ember kept speed-walking out of the Progress Towers straight for her scooter, leaving Wade trailing behind.

"Ember!" Wade exclaimed. "What's going on?"

"I can't believe she basically offered me a job!" Ember shouted in frustration.

"I know! Could be cool!" Wade scrambled to keep up.

"Yeah, *super* cool, Wade." Ember wheeled around and threw up her arms sarcastically. "I could move out and make glass in a faraway city. Do whatever I want!" Even as she said it, the impossibility of those words was cruel.

Wade shook his head, looking completely befuddled. "I don't understand."

"Argh!" Ember screamed. Of course *he* wouldn't. Wade just floated from job to job. He *could* go anywhere and *could* do whatever he wanted. There was nothing stopping him. But Ember's path had been set long before. One dinner in the Water District wasn't going to change that.

She snapped on her helmet and revved her scooter. "I'm going home."

"Fine," Wade said, looking hurt but determined. "Then I'm going with you."

Before she could stop him, Wade hopped on the back of her scooter. She floored it, zipping off into the night with Wade clinging to the seat for dear life behind her.

"Look, my mom was just trying to be helpful!" Wade cried as they careened through the streets. His water sloshed with every twist and turn. "She doesn't know how excited you are to run the shop!"

"Arrrrgh!" Ember's temper roiled. She gunned the engine even harder.

"What is the matter?" Wade screamed, trying not to fall off.

"Nothing!" Ember snapped.

"Yeah?" Wade retorted. "Because we're going, like, a thousand—
BUS!"

Ember dipped the scooter to the right just in time, avoiding a
head-on collision with a bus on the bridge by a hairsbreadth.

"You don't know me, Wade. Okay?" she shouted. "So stop pretend-
ing like you do!"

Ember couldn't see Wade's face, but she was sure he was hurt.

"What is this about?" he asked desperately.

"Nothing!" Ember shouted. "Everything! I don't know. It's—"

Feeling like she was going to explode, Ember slammed on the
brakes, skidding to a stop outside the Fireplace. She breathed
heavily. Her head hurt. Everything inside her hurt. Why did this
all have to be so hard?

"I don't think I actually *do* want to run the shop, okay?" She
forced the words out, guilt-ridden at the blasphemy. "*That's* what
my temper has been trying to tell me."

Ember thought about all those days working in the shop: praying to the Blue Flame that *this* was the day she would finally keep
her cool, panicking every time she felt the rage rumbling inside
her, and later resigning herself to the fact that she'd just have to
try again the next day. She thought about how, before this week,
she'd rarely even left Firetown. "I'm trapped."

She got off the scooter. Wade looked at her like he didn't know what to say.

"You know what's crazy?" She laughed. "Even when I was a *kid*, I would pray to the Blue Flame to be good enough to fill my father's shoes someday. Because this place is his dream. But I never once . . ." Her voice broke. "I never once asked what *I* wanted to do. I think that's because deep down I knew it didn't matter."

Ember looked at Wade, waiting for his reaction. But for the first time since she'd known him, he didn't have the answers.

"EMBER LUMEN!"

Her mother's voice rang out behind them, and Ember nearly stopped breathing.

Oh, flame.

"Don't move!" Cinder shouted, running up to them.

Ember had to figure a way out of this. Fast.

"Mom, it's okay!" she said quickly. "He's just a friend."

"I could smell you from over there!" Cinder fumed. "You *stink!*"

Ember was baffled. "What are you talking about?"

"*You* know what I'm talking about!" Her mother jabbed her finger accusingly, glaring from Wade to Ember. "I've seen the picture of eyeballs under your notebook. You stink every time you look at it! But I never thought it was a Water guy!"

Realization dawning on her, Ember sniffed her arm. "You're smelling *love* on me?" She glanced at Wade. Did she . . . ? What? No. She couldn't . . . *Was* she?

"If your father finds out . . ." Cinder looked like she might turn purple herself. "Fire and Water cannot be together! I'll prove it! Come with me."

Wade had never been in Ember's mom's smoke-reading room. The air in here felt hazy and thick, like a richly perfumed cloud.

Ember's mom still looked furious. She slammed two sticks down on the table between them.

"I'll splash this on your heart to bring love to the surface," she snapped. With an angry flick, she splattered some oil on Ember. Then she did the same to Wade, the oil mixing and swirling inside him. He flinched, thinking the oil would be hot. But once it hit him, he realized it was kind of like popcorn butter, slimy but not unpleasant. "Ooh," he said.

Ember's mom pointed to the two sticks. "And then you must light these with your fire, and I'll read the smoke."

Beside him, Ember lit her stick. She kept sniffing her arm. Meanwhile, Wade looked at his stick uncertainly. "Uhhh . . ."

"Hah! See, Ember?" Her mom sat back and folded her arms smugly. "It cannot be."

Wade turned to Ember and shrugged. Her mom was right. There was no way for him to light the stick. He couldn't help feeling disappointed. Though Water people never did smoke readings—for good reason—he'd been anxious to see what the smoke would say. Did Ember really love him? Because *he* knew how he felt about her. If he was being honest, he'd known since the moment he met her. No one had ever given him hope and purpose like she had. She was special, like a light guiding him through the dark. He didn't need a smoke reading to tell him: he loved Ember Lumen.

But right now, sitting in this room with the dizzying scent of incense saturating his senses, there wasn't much he could do to prove it. He couldn't light the stick. At least not on his own.

"Actually . . ." He looked at Ember's beautiful flame, and a sudden thought bubble occurred to him. Ignoring Ember's bewildered look, he stood in front of her, facing the stick, and lifted his shirt just enough for her light to refract through his liquid torso like a sunbeam through a magnifying glass. He aimed the beam at the top of the stick. It began to smoke—and then it ignited!

"Whoa . . ." Ember and her mom said at the same time.

The trio watched as the smoke rose, spiraling up toward the ceiling like a double helix. Ember's mom leaned in closer to sniff the smoke, and Wade held his breath. This was the moment of truth.

"Cinder! Who's down there?"

Ember gasped in horror. "It's my dad. You have to go!"

"Wait!" Wade whispered urgently as Ember and Cinder rushed him out of the reading room and to the shop door. They both looked ashen at the prospect of what would happen should Ember's dad catch him. But all of Wade's thoughts lingered on the double helix of smoke. What had it meant?

"Are we a match?" he asked.

Ember's mom didn't answer. They shooed him out the door.

"Go!" Ember insisted. "He can't catch you here!"

"But—" Wade spluttered. He couldn't leave—not now!

"Go." Ember's eyes were pleading. "I'll—I'll find you later. I promise."

Chapter 27

Ember and her mom wheeled toward Bernie. The front door had just clicked behind them. Ember prayed that her àshfá hadn't seen anything.

"What's going on?" Bernie asked, coughing slightly. "I woke up and no one was upstairs."

"Oh, it, uh, was just me." Ember scrambled for an excuse. "I came down to double-check the locks. And Mom came down."

"Yes, and we . . . began looking at this door. We don't talk about this door enough!" Cinder shouted.

Ember shot her mom a look as Bernie eyed them curiously.

"Well, since you are awake . . ." Bernie broke into a huge grin. "I was going to tell you tomorrow, but I am too excited to sleep. In two days, I retire!"

Ember's flame flickered.

"Oh, Bernie!" Cinder exclaimed, rushing forward to hug him.

"Two days?" Ember repeated. Her throat had gone dry.

"Yes!" Bernie cried. "We are going to throw a *big* party! A grand reopening! That way, I can tell the whole world my *daughter* is taking over!"

Bernie whirled Cinder around the store in an impromptu dance as though they were a youthful Fire couple again.

But Ember felt sick to her stomach. Two days. Her àshfá was retiring in *two days*? Ember couldn't keep up, everything around her was changing so fast.

Two days earlier, taking over the Fireplace was her heart's greatest desire.

Two hours earlier, every choice she'd ever made had been cast into doubt.

And in two days' time, the shop would be her future. Permanently.

"I have a gift for you, Ember!" Bernie suddenly exclaimed. He rushed to the counter and pulled out a large box covered with dust. "I've had this for a while. After our talk, I know now is the time. But before I give it to you, I need you to understand what it means to me."

Bernie's expression turned serious as he looked at Ember. "When I left Fire Land," he began, "I gave my father the *Bà Ksô*. The Big

Bow. It is the highest form of respect. But . . . my father did not return the Bow. He did not give me his blessing."

Bernie hung his head, reliving the painful memory. "He said if we left Fire Land, we would lose who we are. They never got to see all of this." He gestured wide to the shop. "They didn't get to see that I *never* forgot we are Fire. This is the burden I still carry."

Cinder comforted her husband. Ember, meanwhile, felt wretched. She didn't know what to say.

"Ember, it is important that you know you have *my* blessing every day you come in here," Bernie told her. "So I had this made for you."

He opened the large box, revealing a brand-new sign for the shop. Ember recognized it at once. Her àshfá must have seen one of the designs doodled in her notebook, because it was an exact match. *Ember's Fireplace* blazoned across the vibrant orange sign, ensuring that it would be visible all around Firetown.

"Àshfá." Ember's voice broke. Her àshfá's eyes were shining with happiness and pride. It was everything she had ever hoped for. "That means so much."

Bernie flared brighter than Ember had seen in many years. "It's going to be *big*!" he whooped. "Bright! Everyone is going to see this. Ember's Fireplace! We'll unveil it at the grand reopening!"

"Come, Bernie." Cinder took his hand before he could get too worked up. "You need your rest." She shot Ember a meaningful look, then led Bernie back up the stairs.

Ember remained alone, standing in the center of the shop, staring at the sign.

Everything she'd ever wanted was right there before her, resting on the countertop at her fingertips.

Why, oh, why couldn't this have happened a week earlier, before she'd met Wade? Before he'd flooded into her life and changed everything?

Her hand grazed the glass Vivisteria sphere in her pocket, its weight suddenly, intrusively heavy.

She knew what she had to do.

Silently, Ember sank to the floor and began to cry.

Chapter 28

"Ember! Oh my gosh, I was so worried!" Wade was beyond relieved to see Ember standing outside his mom's apartment door. It had been almost a full day since the smoke-reading fiasco, and he hadn't heard anything from her. No message. No signal. He'd been getting ready to return to the Fireplace himself, consequences be darned.

"Are you okay? What did your mom say? About our reading?" His questions came flooding out all at once.

But Ember just shook her head. "Nothing. Look, I have a gift for you."

Ember held out a small simple box. Wade opened it. Inside was the gleaming glass Vivisteria sphere.

"And you came all the way here to give it to me?" Wade asked, touched by the gesture. But the sad look in Ember's eyes told him something was wrong. "Wait—why are you giving me gifts?"

Ember looked away, and Wade's stomach plummeted. This wasn't a gift. It was a goodbye.

"Oh, no," he pleaded. "Oh, no, no, no, no." He didn't know what her parents had said to her, but he couldn't lose Ember—not now! Not when he was almost certain she felt the same way about him that he did about her.

"Hold on!" he said desperately. "I think I have something to show you." An idea to help Ember had occurred to Wade earlier that week after their hot-air balloon ride. It was kind of crazy and he wasn't even sure it would work, so he hadn't mentioned anything. But given the circumstances, it was now or never.

"Just give me two seconds," he implored her. "I have to call Gale. And you're going to need a pair of boots!"

An hour later, Ember stood with Wade at the place she had gone with her àshfá years earlier. Before them stood Garden Central Station, only it was a ghost of the palatial terminal Ember had once marveled at. Most of the building's facade had crumbled over time, forming piles of rubble around the perimeter. Fences and caution tape warned people to keep out. But even those had fallen to disrepair. No one bothered coming to this decrepit station anymore. It was a blight in the center of the city too expensive to demolish, so it simply remained abandoned. Ironically, a worn sign that read *No Fire Allowed* still hung crookedly at the front door.

"Wade, what are we doing here?" Ember asked.

"Just follow me!" Wade insisted. His eyes shone abnormally bright.

He led her into the darkened terminal, and Ember's fire cast strange shadows on the crumbling tile walls. Up ahead, a staircase that led down into the central atrium of the station was flooded, eerily still dark water pooled all the way to the top.

"Hey! It's my favorite fireball!"

Ember recognized the familiar face standing by the edge of the flooded staircase holding a flashlight. "Hey, Gale," she said, even more confused now. "What's . . . what's going on?"

"Okay, hear me out," Wade said. "I know you think you have to end this, but . . ." He pointed to the staircase. "See that flooded tunnel? It goes to the main terminal. Do you still want to see a Vivisteria?"

Ember blinked. Was he serious?

Wade nodded to Gale, and she began blowing an air bubble in the water flooding the staircase. The bubble grew enormous in size, large enough to hold—

"Wait." Understanding dawned on Ember. "I'm supposed to get *in* there?"

"The air should last . . ." Wade said.

"At least twenty minutes," Gale finished.

But Ember wasn't sure she was ready for this. Even with fire-proof boots, what if the bubble popped? Just the thought of it made Ember's flame run cold. As much as she wanted to see a Vivisteria flower, she didn't want to *die* for it.

But Wade wasn't going to be deterred. "*They* said you couldn't go in there," he insisted, pointing to another NO FIRE ALLOWED sign. "Why does *anyone* get to tell you what you can do in your life?"

Ember stared at the bubble. Gale held it open at the ready, nodding confidently. She was a city supervisor, so she must know what she was doing . . . right?

In the darkness, Ember could see her own reflection in Wade's face. The reflection of a young Fire woman who had dreamed all her life of seeing a single flower. This was her chance.

Ember took several deep breaths. "Okay." She tried to pump herself up. "Let's do this."

Gale breathed an extra blast of air into the bubble for good measure . . .

Ember took a huge breath . . .

And she jumped in.

Bub-wub-bub-wubble!

The bubble wobbled and stretched under her weight, elongating in the water.

But after a moment, it settled, and Ember stood with her arms out, perfectly balanced within the protective sphere. It had worked! This was incredible—Wade's idea was going to work!

With a grin of disbelief, she flashed Wade two thumbs up as Gale sealed up the top of the bubble. Then Wade jumped in beside her and began to swim, pushing the bubble with Ember safely inside deeper into the murky abyss.

Chapter 29

Ember had never experienced anything like this in her entire life. The absence of light under the water was absolute—a thick, oppressive shroud obscuring all detail. Yet, as they swam deeper, Ember dared to flare her fire a bit more brightly. Her bubble became a shining sphere illuminating the depths, the first light to touch any of these surfaces in decades. And as they exited the long tunnel and emerged into the water-filled atrium of Garden Central Station, Ember gasped.

It was like swimming back in time. Everything there remained untouched, miraculously preserved underwater. Opulent tiled mosaics stretched across the walls. Carved archways stood watch over tunnels that led to old train platforms, long since closed.

And in the center of it all, two twisting green vines spiraled up toward the ceiling in a double helix. The Vivisteria tree—preserved, but flowerless.

Wade pushed Ember closer, and her light touched the plant.

Incredibly, the plant reacted to her glow, and a small, precious Vivisteria bud blossomed.

"A Vivisteria." Ember breathed. Her chest rose and fell with emotion. In that moment, she was five years old again: just a little spark who had read a poem and still thought the entire world was hers to explore.

Ember gazed up at the towering plant and flared her light with all her might, casting brilliant, colorful caustics around the entire underwater ballroom. Wade pushed her bubble higher, and every spot that her light touched burst with magnificent Vivisteria blooms growing purple and red and fuchsia.

Together, Fire and Water, they swam through the vines, Wade dazzled by the colors and Ember reaching out toward the beauty that was just a thin bubble's film away from her touch. Her eyes prickled with tears. After a lifetime of waiting, that was more than close enough.

Suddenly, she felt a stabbing prick on the top of her head. "Ouch!"

She looked up and her eyes grew wide. The bubble was shrinking—it had reached the flames on her head and was growing smaller by the second.

"Oh, no!" Wade exclaimed, realizing what was happening. "You're running out of air!" He immediately began swimming her bubble toward a staircase leading up to the surface.

Inside, Ember began to panic. How far down were they? Could they make it back in time? What if Wade didn't know how to get back out? She started hyperventilating, consuming the precious little air that much faster.

"Hang on," Wade urged her. "We're almost there. Try to breathe slow and steady."

Hunched down and clutching her knees, Ember looked at Wade. His face was determined, and his gaze focused ahead. He looked steady and strong, just like he had that night when he heaved sandbags against the culvert with incredible strength. Knowing he was there with her gave Ember the courage to stay calm. She slowed her breath, even as the walls of the bubble grew tighter around her.

Around a corner and up a staircase. Time was running out. Wade swam at top speed, pushing with all his might. Ember squeezed herself smaller, closing her eyes but still breathing slow.

Then . . .

Fwoosh!

They burst through the surface at the top of a long staircase leading out toward Mineral Lake. The moment her bubble hit the air, it popped, sending Ember tumbling onto the ground. Wade collapsed beside her, breathing hard. But they had done it. Ember was safe.

"Are you okay?" Wade pushed himself up and rushed to Ember's side. "I'm so sorry. I never should have—"

"Are you kidding?" Ember leapt to her feet. "That was amazing! I finally saw a Vivisteria!" She beamed at Wade, bursting with joy.

"It was inspiring," Wade replied mistily. "You were inspiring."

Ember locked eyes with him, losing herself in the sparkle of his gaze. This incredible, crazy, goofy Water man who made the impossible possible.

Then Wade reached his hand out to her. Ember gasped.

"No, Wade," she said, wishing with every fiber in her being that she could. "We can't touch."

"Maybe we can," Wade insisted.

"No." Ember shook her head.

"But can't we just prove it?" Wade asked. "Let's see what happens, and if it's a disaster, then we'll know this would never work."

"But it actually *could* be a disaster." Ember tried to make him see reason. "I could vaporize you. You could extinguish me."

"Let's start small," Wade said.

The way he held his hand out toward hers with such confidence, Ember couldn't help being drawn in. After all they had been through together, something in his eyes made her hope—believe—that this was possible.

With a deep breath, Ember hesitantly extended her hand over his. She lowered it closer, and his water started to boil. Instantly, she pulled away, thinking she had burned him. But Wade held her gaze reassuringly and stretched his hand out again. Very slowly, Ember matched her palm to his, and they pressed their hands together.

They both gasped at the touch. Ember's hand steamed and Wade's hand boiled, but the longer they pressed their palms together, the more their chemistry equalized, finding a balance. Carefully, they stepped closer, the stability of Wade's water counterbalancing the strength of Ember's heat.

Ember couldn't believe it. It *was* possible. She felt safe. And happy.

Wade leaned in close, lost in the moment. "I'm so lucky."

Those words—they scorched Ember like a searing bolt of lightning. A flashback of her àshfá, tired, weary, struggling to repair the broken shop, flashed through her head. *I'm so lucky I have you,* he had told her.

Ember gasped and pulled away. What was she thinking? This was wrong—she was being selfish. A bad daughter. She had come to *break up* with Wade. Not accidentally, maybe, possibly, fall in—

No! She was scheduled to take over the shop in one day's time. One day's time! Her father was counting on her to carry on his *dream.* And what was she doing? She was with a Water guy, imagining a life that would crush her parents. After all they had been through—after everything her àshfá had sacrificed and entrusted to her—what right did she have to even consider leaving all that?

"I have to go," she said hurriedly, rushing toward the Mineral Lake train stop on the other side of the shore.

"Wait, what?" Wade asked in utter confusion. "Where are you going?"

"Back to my life at the shop," Ember said firmly. "Where I belong. I take over tomorrow."

"Whoa, whoa, whoa, hold up!" Wade tried to block her path. "You don't *want* that. You said it yourself."

"It doesn't matter what I want," Ember told him.

"Of course it does!" Wade said more forcefully than Ember had ever heard from him. "You've got an opportunity to do something you *want* with your life!"

"Want?!" Ember glared at him. Shame and fury burned in her eyes. "Yeah, that may work in your 'follow your heart' family. But getting to do what you want is a luxury. And not for people like me."

"Why not?" Wade implored. "Just tell your father how you feel. This is too important. Maybe he'll agree."

"Oh, yeah. Hah." Ember rolled her eyes and started up the train stairs.

"Funny." Wade called after her. "And this whole time I thought you were so strong. But it turns out you're just afraid."

Ember blazed near purple. Wade's words cut deep. "Don't you *dare* judge me." Her voice shook with anger. "You don't know what it's like to have parents who gave up *everything* for you. I'm *Fire*, Wade. I can't be anything more than that. It's what I am and what my *family* is. It's our way of life. I cannot throw all that away *just for you*."

A train pulled into the station. Ember backed toward the doors as Wade shook his head.

"I don't understand," he said miserably.

"And that alone is a reason this could never work." Ember boarded the train, steeling herself even though inside she was falling apart. "It's over, Wade."

Chapter 30

Back at home, Wade collapsed onto his waterbed, spreading out into a thin puddle as he commanded the home sound system to play "Lonely Is the Water Man Without Love." On repeat.

The sad strains of the unrequited love song echoed over the ceiling speakers, and Wade bawled. He bawled and bawled. He had never felt so heartbroken in his entire life. Wade wished he could simply sink into the bed and disappear. So he did, letting his eyes float on the surface like two tearful bubbles.

"Wade, honey, are you okay?" His mom knocked on the door. When she came in and saw Wade all puddled up, her eyes grew teary, too. "Oh, my sweet baby boy." She hurried to the edge of the bed. "What's the matter?"

"Ember ... broke ... up ... with ... me!" Wade choked the words out between sobs.

His mom gasped. "No! But why? You both looked so happy together. And I thought you said her mom smelled love on her? What went wrong?"

"I don't know!" Wade wailed. He tearfully told his mother everything. About Ember giving the Vivisteria sphere to him. About their incredible journey into the flooded Garden Central Station and the magical way the Vivisteria plant had blossomed in her light. How they were able to touch. And finally, how Ember had suddenly changed her mind and broken his heart, saying she couldn't throw everything away "just" for him.

His mom listened to it all, patting her poor son's puddle head the whole time. "I'm so sorry, sweetie. It sounds like Ember has a lot of conflicted feelings right now."

"What about *my* feelings?" Wade popped his head up. "I love her, Mom! I did everything I could think of to show her how I feel, and she still shot me down."

"Did you tell her you love her?" his mom asked.

"Not exactly." Wade's lower lip quivered. "I wanted to, but I didn't get the chance. And I wasn't sure how she felt."

"Wade, I saw the way she looked at you during the Crying Game," Brook told him. "We all saw it. She cried tears of fire, for heaven's sake. She's in love with you, too, bubblekins."

"Then why did she leave me?" Wade asked.

"Sometimes it's not as simple as just knowing how you feel." His mom sighed. "Love is hard. It takes work." She thought for a moment. "Did I ever tell you how I fell in love with your father?"

Wade sniffled and re-formed to sit up on the bed beside his mom. "He saw you sketching on the side of the waveball field," Wade recalled. "He said he'd never seen anyone more beautiful, and he told his teammates right then and there that he was going to marry you."

Brook laughed, her eyes shining bright. "That's how *he* fell in love with me. Your father was very determined. He knew what he wanted, and he didn't let anything stop him. And that was the problem. See, I didn't want to be with someone who thought he already knew *all* the answers. I wanted someone spontaneous—someone who wasn't afraid to admit when they'd made a mistake. I wanted someone to share the journey with."

"I'm not sure I understand." Wade shrugged.

"Your father had a never-ending river of confidence," Brook continued. "He was all about victory. Winning the game. Earning the trophy. He always had to be right." Brook chuckled. "He was the most stubborn man I'd ever met. But he had a huge heart. I saw that. And the day I fell in love with him was the day that he admitted he was scared."

"Scared?" Wade asked.

"Mmm-hmm." Brook nodded. "He told me he was scared of messing things up. That he wasn't sure I could love someone like him. It terrified him. That was when I knew he was a bigger man than all his victories on the field. He was strong enough to allow us to grow together, as a family."

Wade wiped his nose on his shirt. "But I never told Ember I had all the answers," he insisted. "I did everything I could think of to show her she was strong on her own." His eyes welled with fresh tears. "But none of it was good enough. *I* wasn't good enough! It was all for nothing!"

Brook rocked Wade in her arms as he cried. "Oh, my bubble pumpkin," she said soothingly. "Your father was always so worried about you. He was afraid he'd failed you somehow, hadn't given you enough direction."

"He wanted me to be like him," Wade said a little bitterly.

"Oh, no," his mother insisted. "He always wanted you to be *you*. Just the best version of yourself that you could be. But he knew that would take hard work. And, I think we can both agree, choosing a path and sticking with it has always been hard for you."

"Ember made me feel like I had a path," Wade said sadly. "She made me want to try."

"Then *work* for her love," Brook urged him. "Don't give up. Don't let her give up on you. It sounds like she's under an incredible amount of pressure. But maybe she needs to see how she's changed *you* in order to feel brave enough to change herself."

Wade mulled that over for a minute. He was still pretty upset that Ember had rejected him—twice—after everything they had been through. Her words by the lake had been harsh. But he also knew what it felt like to be scared and to say mean things because, even though you knew the other person was right, you weren't sure you were strong enough to do what they were asking. He knew the shame of letting someone down and never having the opportunity to set things right. Maybe Ember felt that way right now. But the difference was, he was still here. The opportunity wasn't lost.

"She's taking over the store tomorrow," he said thoughtfully.

"Sounds like you should talk to her before then," Brook said.

Wade gave a final sniffle. "Do you really think she loves me?"

"Only one way of finding out." Brook winked. "But yes, I'm sure."

"Thanks, Mom." Wade hugged his mother so tight her water squished. Then he stood up and flexed his arms. "Okay, Fire shop . . . place . . . people. Watch out. Because Wade's coming to town!"

He changed the song to "Eye of the Tiger Fish" on maximum volume. The entire apartment vibrated with the force of the music, and Brook wiped a tear from her eye. "Oh, my little drip, drip baby has grown into such a strong man. Your father would be so proud."

Chapter 31

Strings of fire lights on ropes crisscrossed the street in front of the Fireplace. Bernie and Cinder were adjusting crimson banners along a stage. Tables were set with richly woven placemats and platters piled high with kol nuts and hot logs and smoked pine chips. All of Firetown had gathered for the occasion. This was a huge deal: the little shop that had started it all was finally changing hands to the new generation.

Ember watched from the side of the stage, dressed in ornate traditional robes made of multicolored metals and jewels. She took a deep breath. This was it. It was really happening. Everything she had worked toward for so long was coming true tonight. A small lava bead trickled down her temple as she gazed out on the crowd of Fire people. Everyone seemed so excited. There was the Sol family with their little baby, who was sucking down a bottle of lighter fluid. And over in the corner were the shop regulars, for once not cracking jokes at Ember's expense. Everyone that mattered to her all congregated in one place to watch as she—Ember Lumen—made her family proud.

Everyone except one person.

With a twinge, she imagined catching sight of Wade's Water head poking up from the crowd. But the thought was fleeting, and she pushed it aside. She knew everything she'd said to him. She'd seen the hurt on his face. Even if she hadn't really meant it—even if she longed for the coolness of his hand pressed against hers—she tried to believe that this right here was what she was meant to do.

"Just take deep breaths," she told herself. "After tonight, everything will be fine."

A vision of the Vivisteria flower flashed through her mind. At least that was one small piece of fantasy she could hold onto, tucked away in the corner of her mind as she fulfilled her familial duty.

Bernie emerged from the shop holding a lantern with the sacred Blue Flame. Ember prayed, "Please, Blue Flame, help me to be happy."

"Everyone, welcome!" Bernie announced. "It is good to see your faces. I am honored to have served you." He bowed, and everyone in the audience clapped.

"But it is time to move on," he continued. He motioned for Ember to join him onstage, and she stepped up beside him. "My daughter," Bernie said to her, "you are the ember of our family fire. That is why I am so proud to have you take over my life's work."

Bernie dramatically touched a rope leading up to a tarp covering something at the top of the Fireplace building. It ignited like a fuse, setting the tarp ablaze and engulfing the whole store in a ball of fire. The crowd oohed, mesmerized. When the flame subsided, a new sign was proudly revealed above the store with blazing letters that read *Ember's Fireplace*.

"Pretty good trick, huh?" Bernie winked at Ember as the audience cheered.

Ember gazed at the sign. It felt so strange seeing her name up there. She should be proud. *Everyone* was proud. Why couldn't she just feel proud?

Cinder motioned for quiet, and the audience settled. Bernie carefully picked up the Blue Flame lantern. "This is a lantern I had brought from the old country," he proclaimed. "Today, I pass it on to you."

Ember and her àshfá locked eyes as he reverently held the lantern out, prepared for her to grasp its handle.

Ember took a deep breath. This was it. There was no going back now. She hesitated for just a moment, then squared her shoulders and reached out. She accepted this life—and everything that went with it.

"I thought of other reasons!" someone called out.

Everyone whipped around in their seats to see who it was.

Ember's heart skipped a beat.

"Wade?"

The lone Water man strode forward through the crowd heroically, right up to the stage.

"Oh, boy," Cinder mumbled under her breath.

"What are you *doing* here?" Ember asked, flabbergasted.

"You said me not understanding is the reason we could never work," Wade continued loudly. "But I thought of other reasons. A bunch of them! Like, number one: you're Fire, I'm Water. I mean, come on, that's crazy, right?"

Bernie looked from Cinder to Ember, completely perplexed. "Who *is* this?"

Cinder shook her head. "No idea."

"Number two!" Wade was focused on Ember. "I'm crashing your party. Like, what kind of jerk am I?"

"A pretty big one," Ember muttered.

"Right?" Wade held his arms wide in mock agreement. "Number three: I can't eat your delicious foods!" He grabbed a kol nut from a nearby table and popped the sizzling delicacy right into his mouth. Instantly, his throat boiled, and the heat blistered up in a steam bubble that popped through the top of his head. Wade grimaced in pain. "*Very* unpleasant!"

"Wait, I know him!" Bernie's eyes flew wide with recognition. "He is the *food inspector!*"

"Oh, right!" Wade nodded. "Number four! I'm *banned* from your father's shop!"

Wade stepped up onstage. Ember couldn't help giving him her full attention.

"There are a million reasons why this can't work," he said. "A million nos. But there's also one yes. We *touched.*" Wade stepped closer. "And when we did, something happened to us. Something *impossible.* We changed each other's chemistry."

Ember couldn't take her eyes off his. She couldn't believe Wade was here. That those sparkling, hopeful, dazzlingly blue eyes could even look at her after everything she had said. After all the hurt she had caused him.

"Enough!" Bernie stepped in between them. "What kind of food inspection is this?"

"A food inspection of the heart, sir!" Wade declared.

Bernie looked like he was going to explode. "Who *are* you?"

"Just a guy who burst into your daughter's life in a flooded old basement." Wade was so close to Ember, she could have reached out to take his hand.

"So you *are* the one who burst the pipes!" Bernie said accusingly.

"What? Not me," Wade countered without thinking. "It was . . ."

Ember's heart nearly stopped. She shook her head almost imperceptibly as Wade's eyes involuntarily darted to her. Wade must have picked up on her signal, because he tried to cover. But it was too late. Bernie had seen. And he understood.

"You?" Bernie asked Ember, betrayal washing over his face. "*You* burst the pipe?"

"I–I," Ember stammered.

"Ember," Wade tried to help her.

"SILENCE!" Bernie roared.

But Wade roared back. "NO! Ember—take the chance! Let your father know who you really are."

But Ember couldn't speak. She was frozen in panic.

Wade looked deep into her eyes. "Look, I had regrets when my dad died. But because of you, I've learned to 'embrace the light while it burns.' *Tishók'.*" He pronounced the Firish word perfectly. "You don't have forever to say what you need to say. I love you, Ember Lumen."

The audience gasped. Everyone gasped.

Ember could barely breathe.

"And I'm pretty sure you love me, too," Wade finished.

Ember looked from her àshfá to Wade. She wasn't sure she could bear this. No matter what she did now, she was going to hurt someone she loved. She could feel herself shutting down.

"No, Wade," she said, willing up a wall of flame to guard her emotions. "I don't."

"That's not true!" Cinder burst forward into the center of the bizarre drama unfolding. "I did their reading!"

Again, the audience gasped. The shop regulars ate a few kol nuts like pieces of popcorn.

"Bernie, it's love," Cinder promised. "It's true love."

But Ember shook her head. "No, Mom. You're wrong. Wade—you have to go."

"But, Ember," Wade pleaded, trying to reconnect with her.

"I DON'T LOVE YOU!" Ember flared. She panted, her insides wrenching. "Go," she told Wade definitively.

Wade looked like he might be absorbed right down into the ground and trickle away. The hurt in his eyes was tangible. Slowly, he pulled the glass Vivisteria sphere out from his pocket and placed it on the stage. Then he left.

Ember watched him go. She couldn't think straight anymore. She was drowning.

"You have been seeing *Water?*" Bernie's voice seared through the silence.

Ember winced. "Àshfá, I—"

"You caused the leak in the shop!?" Bernie fell into a coughing fit, but he refused to stop talking. "I . . . TRUSTED . . . YOU!"

Ember didn't know what to say. The truth was out there, hanging in the air. And yet she was still too cowardly to confess.

"You will *not* take over the shop!" Bernie hacked and snatched up the Blue Flame lantern. "I will no longer retire!"

He thundered back inside. Cinder rushed after him, calling his name with worry.

Ember stood there, devastated. Everything was ruined. It was all her fault. She had failed everyone.

Meanwhile, the people in the audience weren't certain what they were supposed to do. No one seemed to want to go near Ember—that was for sure. One by one, the guests filtered away, ultimately leaving Ember alone onstage.

Numbly, she picked up the glass Vivisteria sphere and put it into her pocket. Then she walked over to her scooter, climbed on, and drove away.

Chapter 32

High on the bridge overlooking downtown Element City, Ember gazed miserably out at the horizon. Buildings glittered like a million sparks against the dark night sky. *It would take an act of God to get me to cross that bridge,* she remembered telling Clod only a week ago. Now even an act of God couldn't fix the mess she'd made.

The waves on the bay were rough tonight, splashing with white foam against the sandy shore. A memory flashed through Ember's mind—she and Wade holding hands by the lake. Even the happiest moment of her life had been wrong—all wrong.

Why can't I just be a good daughter? she thought sadly. Reaching into her pocket, she withdrew the glass Vivisteria sphere and studied it for a moment. Then she drew her arm back to heave it into the water. The last reminder of how selfish she'd been and all the pain she'd caused her family.

Only . . . she couldn't do it. Her arm hovered in the air, unable to let go.

"I really am trapped." She wanted desperately to be a good daughter. But she also wasn't ready to let go of what might have been. She couldn't choose. And her indecision was hurting the people she loved. "I can't . . . I can't do anything right."

A sudden burst of light glimmered in the distance. Ember wouldn't have paid much attention, except it was directly where she and Wade had flown the hot-air balloon just a few days ago. Out by the culvert they had sealed together.

She watched the light, furrowing her brow. That was weird. The glimmer was shifting. It almost looked like moonlight reflecting off . . .

"Water." Ember sucked in her breath. "The glass—it broke. Oh, no, no, no, no."

With horror, Ember watched a growing wall of water rushing down the main canal, no longer held back by the tempered glass barrier she had created. The deluge snaked through the main part of the city, right toward—

"Firetown," Ember whispered.

She grabbed her scooter and streaked off at top speed.

The flood would reach her parents any minute.

"Well, this is it." Wade tearfully held up a train ticket. "One-way ticket to anywhere but here."

Standing across from him on the station platform just beyond the bridge to Firetown was his entire family. Everyone sobbed uncontrollably.

"Go!" His mother dabbed her eyes with a soaked handkerchief. "Travel the world. Heal that broken heart." She embraced Wade and rocked him back and forth as she wept. "My little drip, drip baby boy. Drip, drip, drip goes the baby boy."

"I made you a painting." Harold sniffled and handed Wade his latest artwork. "It's of a lonely man awash in sadness."

Wade admired the painting. It was a portrait of himself, standing at the train station ticket counter purchasing his one-way ticket. Harold must have painted it on the spot.

Wade bawled.

His mom bawled.

Alan and Eddy and Lake and Ghibli and Marco and Polo and Harold all bawled.

A worker came over with a CAUTION, WET FLOOR sign. He placed it beside their pools of tears, causing the Ripple family to cry all the more.

Just then, a train whistle blared. It was time for Wade to go.

He gave a final sad look out toward Firetown. Somewhere in that smoky village was the love of his life. But . . . he would never see her again.

The tears in his eyes must have been misting his vision, because everything looked hazy.

He rubbed his eyes and looked again.

All of Firetown still looked fuzzy in the distance, like it was covered with clouds. Or—

"Steam." Wade felt his water run cold.

One by one, the Firetown lights were blinking out.

"Ember."

Chapter 33

"Mom! Dad!" Ember zoomed up to the shop. The water level in the streets was already rising, causing her scooter to hydroplane. Water splashed up and seared her legs.

She couldn't believe the chaotic sight before her eyes. All throughout Firetown, people were scrambling to get to higher ground. One wave of water after another rushed up against the buildings and washed over vehicles and vendor carts. Everywhere she looked, steam rose in a thick fog as lights extinguished along the streets.

"Mom!" Ember screamed, leaping off her scooter and onto the roof of a half-submerged vehicle. Her parents were floating helplessly on the stage from the ceremony. It had been lifted by the rising water like a raft. They were safe as long as they stayed afloat. But her àshfá was struggling against Cinder in a panic.

"The flame!" he cried. "Let me go!"

Ember whipped around to look at the Fireplace. The glow of the Blue Flame still burned inside. But two feet of water was already pressing up against the front door. It was only a matter of time before the door gave way and the whole place flooded.

Without thinking, Ember leapt from one piece of floating debris to the next, striving to get close enough to the shop to climb in through the transom window above the front door.

"Ember, NO!" she heard her father yell.

But she didn't listen. With a final lunge, she grabbed hold of the transom window and pulled herself up and inside the shop.

Everything rumbled and creaked eerily inside the darkened store. Water spurted through cracks. Pipes shuddered dangerously in the walls.

Ember grabbed sandbags to stand on as she pressed her entire weight against the front door. If she could hold it until the worst of the flood subsided, the shop might be okay. But as the water rose higher outside, covering the entire front window and nearing the open transom, Ember realized it was futile. She couldn't hold the water back—not all on her own.

Without warning, two wide eyes appeared outside the door, pressed against the glass.

Ember nearly jumped back in shock.

"Wade!" she cried in disbelief.

Wade motioned to the handle. "Keemf-holl!" His voice was muffled against the door.

With a rush, Ember realized he was pointing to the door's keyhole. Quickly, she yanked out the key blocking it, and Wade squeezed painfully through, re-forming into his normal shape beside her just as she shoved the key back into place.

"I was hoping to make more of a heroic entrance." He shrugged as he pressed his weight against the door alongside Ember.

But Ember couldn't hide her relief. "You came back." She nearly wept. "After everything I said."

"Are you kidding?" Wade smiled. Ember had never been so grateful to see that beautiful man's smile. "And miss all this?"

Just having Wade beside her bolstered Ember's confidence.

"Hold the door!" she shouted. Then she leapt between the store's shelves and countertops, desperately trying to reach the glowing Blue Flame that sat so exposed in the center of the sacred cauldron. Thinking fast, she snatched up some sandbags and tossed them around the edge of the cauldron before flaring up her fire to melt the sand into a glass barrier that protected the Blue Flame.

Outside, the roar of the flood was deafening. The entire building groaned. Bricks crumbled as pipes burst.

"Ember!" Wade shouted. "We have to go! Now!"

"No!" Ember exclaimed, using her heat to continue forming glass. "I can't leave!"

"I'm sorry to say this, but the shop is done!" Wade yelled. "The flame is done."

"No!" Ember wailed. "This is my father's whole life! I'm not going any—"

Her words were swallowed by a tumult of water crashing through the brick wall and rushing into the shop. Ember stifled a scream as a display shelf crashed into the glass barrier, shattering her work upon impact and cracking the base of the stone cauldron. Water flooded up to the Blue Flame, hissing as it licked the base of the fire.

Ember climbed onto a box before the water could reach her. "Quick! Throw me that lantern!" she cried desperately to Wade.

Wade looked where she was pointing and swam hard toward the empty lantern on the counter. But another violent surge of water rushed in, taking Wade with it. Ember and the Blue Flame cauldron careened toward the old hearth at the back of the store and slammed into it, throwing Ember inside.

"NO!" she cried, somersaulting inside the ash-covered hearth and smacking into the back wall. Meanwhile, debris piled up against the opening, each piece crashing into the other and rising at odd angles, forming a dam. The conglomeration blocked the

entrance to the hearth, preventing the water from coming in—
now. But as Ember pushed herself to her feet, cold dread race
through her. She was sealed in. She couldn't get out.

Ember hung her head. That was when she realized: the Blue
Flame cauldron rested at her feet. Cracked, broken, and empty.
The flame was gone.

"No!" she wailed, covering her mouth with her hand. Not the
Blue Flame, too. She sank to her knees, moaning. "No, no, no, no."
Everything was destroyed. She had failed.

Then, miraculously, a blue glow rose out of the debris.

It was Wade. He was holding the lantern, the sacred Blue Flame
burning safely inside.

"Wade!" she shrieked, rushing forward. She took the lantern
and cradled it like a baby. "Thank you. Thank you."

Ember gazed up at him, her eyes shining bright with relief—and
love. How could she ever have sent away this wonderful, wonderful
man who made the impossible possible just for her?

Suddenly, a sharp pain stabbed her knee. She looked down in
alarm and realized water was starting to seep through the makeshift dam. Quickly, she held her hands out to the debris and heated
it up, sealing the cracks. But the power of her heat had consequences: the hearth she and Wade were trapped in began heating
up as well.

away, starting to sweat. His water boiled all over.

...in here," he gasped.

...y, Ember looked up. The hearth's chimney stack led

...open night sky.

...b!" she shouted.

...gether, they struggled to make their way up the crumbling

...ck walls of the chimney. They had nearly reached the surface

...when—*BAM!*—something smashed into the shop roof, causing the chimney to collapse into itself. Bricks went flying. Their only escape route was sealed shut.

"Back up, back up!" Ember cried urgently, bricks raining down around them.

Side by side, they tumbled back down into the debris-filled hearth. With the only remaining exit destroyed, Ember's fire made the space even hotter. Wade's water boiled precariously fast, steam rising with each tiny bubble burst.

Ember rushed to the hearth's blocked entrance. "I have to open this back up."

"No!" Wade held out a boiling hand to stop her. "The water will come in, and you'll be snuffed out."

"But you're evaporating!" Ember was horrified by how much steam he was releasing. She desperately looked around for

something–anything–to help them. But they were trapped. Th
was no way out–not without one of them . . .

"I–I don't know what to do." Ember's flame flickered.

"Hey." Wade's voice was strangely calm. "It's okay."

"No, it's not okay!" Ember insisted.

But even as he steamed, Wade reached out and took her hand, his boiling water tingling her palm.

"Ember, I have no regrets." He gazed at her adoringly. "You gave me something people search for their whole lives."

"But I can't exist in a world without you." Ember's voice choked with emotion. "I'm sorry I didn't say it before. I love you, Wade."

Truer words had never left Ember's lips. She loved Wade Ripple with all her heart. If holding him would keep him safe, Ember would never let him go. She hadn't meant to hurt him. She'd never wanted to hurt him. She would never forgive herself for that. But now that she finally understood what not just her temper, but her heart, had been telling her all along–how could she lose him?

Ember's fire softened, and her inner prismatic light shone through, casting rainbows along the darkened hearth walls.

Wade's water was barely visible now. He was more vapor than liquid. Still, he smiled.

e it when your light does that."

d Ember, the steam from his body misting around

squeezed her eyes shut. Even as she felt Wade's form
rough her arms, she never wanted to let go.

Chapter 34

"Over here! They're in here!"

Voices echoed outside the hearth. Ember heard something hard slamming into the debris. She wasn't sure how long she'd been trapped in there. Hours. Maybe days. She hadn't been sure she would ever get out. But if she was being honest, she hadn't cared. The thing that mattered most to her in the world was already lost.

Shafts of light shone through as debris fell away under the pounding of sledgehammers. With a mighty *crack*, the entire pile of rubble collapsed.

"Ember!" Her parents rushed forward, embracing their daughter with a startling ferocity.

"Wade is gone," Ember told them, empty. "He saved me."

The weight of those words overwhelmed Ember. Wade had given everything for her. She didn't deserve it. She hadn't deserved him. All she had done was let him down.

Ember could feel her àshfá's eyes on her. She took a deep, shuddering breath and, summoning what little strength she had left inside her, held the Blue Flame lantern out to her father. Being honest with her àshfá terrified her. But she had to be. At least once. For Wade.

"Dad," she said. "This is my fault. The shop—Wade." Her voice broke. "I have to tell you the truth. I don't want to run the shop. I know that was your dream. But it's not mine. I'm sorry." Ember cried. "I'm a bad daughter."

Bernie's eyes sparkled with lava tears as he placed the Blue Flame lantern down on the ground and held his daughter's hands. "Ember, the shop was never the dream," he said. "*You* were the dream. You were always the dream."

Ember collapsed against her àshfá's chest, sobbing as she hugged him. "I loved him, Dad."

Mother, father, and daughter all held one another, crying quietly. They almost didn't hear it at first. The sound was so distant, it seemed more an echo of their own tears. But slowly, faintly, a fourth whimper joined in.

Ember stopped, staying very still, listening. That cry was familiar. Was it possible?

She looked up, and in the light from her fire, something shimmered on the hearth's brick walls. It took Ember a moment to realize what she was seeing. Condensation. Tiny, nearly imperceptible water droplets lining the chimney walls. It couldn't be . . .

"Butterfly," Ember whispered. Then, with impossible hope, she called louder. "Butterfly. Windshield wipers. Half a butterfly."

The cry returned, still soft, but not as distant. A few water droplets fell into a bucket.

Ember's chest swelled. It could be! Because Wade Ripple made the impossible *possible*.

"An old man on his deathbed remembers the summer he fell in love!" she shouted, tears of joy filling her eyes. "She was out of his league, and he was young and scared. He let her go, thinking surely summer would come again. It never did."

Soft weeping filled the hearth, some of the echoes now coming from the bucket of pooled water itself. Cinder realized what was happening and joined in.

"You are a perfect match!" she declared. "Ten out of ten!"

Bernie looked at his wife and daughter in confusion. More drops fell from the ceiling. "I don't understand. What's going on?"

"Just say something to make Water guy cry, okay?" Cinder told him.

"Oh." Bernie cleared his throat. He hesitantly said that Wade was no longer banned from the shop.

Wails resounded around the hearth. Ember stood, energized like never before.

"I want to explore the world with you, Wade Ripple!" she proclaimed, droplets falling all around her. "I want to have you with me, in my life, forever!"

Water poured down, filling the bucket completely. Ember peered in, holding her breath.

There they were. Those two incredible, wonderful, sparkling eyes she knew so well.

Wade stood up from the bucket, re-forming into his normal self, smiling wider than ever.

Ember felt as though she might burst from happiness. She rushed forward to hug Wade, his water immediately counterbalancing her fire, their chemistry connecting. A perfect match.

"I thought I'd lost you." She sobbed tears of joy as he took her face in his hands.

"Can't get rid of me that easily," he replied tenderly. He leaned down to kiss her, and Ember's light shone through his water, refracting off every surface in a spectacular prism of color.

"Whoa," the onlookers murmured. So that was what a *real* Elemental kiss looked like.

Bernie glanced away respectfully. But Cinder slapped his arm.

"I knew it!" she declared. "My nose *always* knows."

Chapter 35

The midday sun burned bright over Firetown, causing Earth, Air, and Water workers alike to wipe their brows. They weren't used to the smoky heat of this part of the city. But friendly Fire folks came out from their patched-up homes, offering them iced lava java and freshly made snacks. And Fire workers who could take the heat frequently swapped in while the others took a break. Rebuilding had taken a while. But little by little, working together, they were almost done.

It had been several months since the flood. As city supervisor, Gale had ordered an immediate construction initiative utilizing every able-bodied worker throughout Element City. The thrum of cement mixers and pounding of jackhammers was everyday background noise in Firetown now. Gale herself, wearing a hard hat, commanded a construction crew.

"I want those underground canals up to *code!*" she shouted as flustered workers scurried back to their diggers. "I had better never see a single *drop* of water above the surface in Firetown, or I'll blow you all above the atmosphere!"

Meanwhile, renovation of the Fireplace was nearly complete. As the foundation of the entire Firetown community, the store site had been granted special historical landmark status. That meant most of the unpermitted structure was grandfathered in.

"Hey, who hasn't skirted a few regulations or two?" Gale had winked to the Lumen family a few weeks prior.

Now Wade and Ember stood in the center of the shop. Ember happily carried boxes of supplies up from the basement. But Wade paced the freshly tiled floor nervously, unable to contain his worry.

"I'm sure you'll get it," he kept repeating over and over. "I mean, you have to get it."

"Wade, relax." Ember shook her head. "If I get it, I get it. If I don't—well, I'll always have a place here."

"But I saw the sample you submitted!" Wade insisted. "It was—wow. Just wow."

He thought back to the glass piece Ember had created for her internship application. It was an intricate mosaic made of brilliant, colorful pieces of glass depicting Firetown and all the people Ember loved. Wade had to hold back tears every time he pictured it. Nothing could represent Ember's creativity, skill, and beauty better than that piece.

"But aren't you supposed to hear back this week?" Wade continued babbling as Ember headed back down to the basement. "Do you think they meant the beginning of the week? Or the end of the week?"

"How is it possible that you're more nervous than I am?" Ember teased. But Wade knew Ember so well now. Maybe better than herself. He could tell by the twinkle in her eye—she was anxious, too.

"I just can't *stand* the waiting!" Wade groaned. "It's so hard not being able to make plans! Not knowing where you're going. When you're going. *If* you're going."

"What's all this about 'if'?" Bernie and Cinder clomped down the basement stairs, holding paint cans and tiles.

"Wade's just worried, Àshfá." Ember rolled her eyes. "I keep telling him, everything will be fine. If the internship doesn't pan out, I can always stay here and help you and Mom."

"Ha!" Bernie flared playfully. "Then you will be helping Clod stack shelves. Because your mother and I are going on vacation no matter what!"

"Oooh!" Wade clapped. He *loved* hearing about travel plans. "Where are you going?"

Bernie eyed Cinder cheekily. "I'll take Ember's mother to the Kol Islands. I hear one week there will make you feel ten years younger." He poked Cinder's arm. "Maybe twenty."

"Ê . . . shútsh!" Cinder shushed him. But Wade couldn't help admiring the warm glow of love between them. It made him wonder if he and Ember would look that happy together when they grew old. He had a feeling they would.

"Àshfá, that's great!" Ember exclaimed. "I'm just sorry it's taken this long. You would have been able to go on vacation years ago if . . . if I hadn't been such a mess."

"Eh, I burn brighter than ever." Bernie flared his fire to show off. "As long as my daughter is happy, I will always burn bright."

Ember flushed beside Wade, and gently, Wade took her hand in his. Her fire tickled his palm as their chemistry equalized. He couldn't wait to start their new life together.

"Knock, knock!" Brook's footsteps splish-splashed down the cellar staircase. "The Ripple clan and I came to drop off some refreshments. I hope you don't mind."

"Not at all," Cinder said graciously. "Please come in. We're sorry the shop is such a mess."

"Oh, don't say that!" Brook's bracelets tinkled along her arm as she waved her hand. She gazed up at the ornamental pipes running along the basement ceiling. "I just love how you're keeping all the original detail, even though the city will be running the water completely underground now."

"Well, those pipes are kind of special." Ember smiled at Wade. "After all, they're where we first met."

A short while later, the Lumen and Ripple families gathered upstairs to enjoy the treats Brook had delivered as well as some Fire Land delicacies.

"Eh—how do you—swallow this?" Bernie tentatively picked up a cube of wobbly jelly. His fire instantly vaporized the cube's moisture, leaving behind a sticky mass.

"You get used to it." Wade burped a heat bubble as he swallowed a kol nut. "It just takes some practice."

Everyone laughed. Then Alan turned to Ember and Wade. "So, have you two figured out where you'll stay when Ember starts the internship?"

"*If* I get the internship," Ember corrected him. "And not yet. But Wade said he has some friends who might know of an apartment for rent."

"Great guys!" Wade slurped up a jelly cube. "I worked with them at a previous job. I wrote them a letter. I'm sure they'll get back to me." Wade thought back to his time at that job—and how he had misplaced some shipments. He gulped. "I hope they'll get back to me."

"Now we just need to wait for the glass company to let me know if I got the internship." Ember shrugged. "I mean, I'm sure they got a ton of applications. I might not even get it."

"Oh, don't say that, honey!" Brook insisted. "Your glassmaking talent is just inspired."

"A real work of art!" Harold added.

"And trust us, we've seen a lot of artists," Lake and Ghibli chimed in.

Ember shrugged, a tiny bit of her prismatic light shining through. "I hope so."

Wade put his arm around her shoulders and gave her a little bubbly squeeze. "I know so."

Just then, the shop phone rang.

Everyone turned to look at it.

Wade nudged Ember hopefully. "You got this."

Slowly, she walked over to receive the call.

Chapter 36

Ember Lumen stood outside the shop, looking up at the newly restored sign hanging over the front door. She breathed in with satisfaction. The graceful, emblazoned letters were scripted just so.

The Fireplace, it read. Not *Ember's Fireplace*. Just *The Fireplace*. It was perfect.

Quietly, she entered the shop, taking in the life thriving within. Not even a year ago, this store had been the only home she'd ever known, a bubble of responsibility she didn't think she could ever leave. And now, well . . .

"Oy! You know what I like best about running this shop?" Flarrietta, who Bernie had hired to take over the shop, shouted to Flarry as they sat behind the counter. They wore fireproof aprons, just like Ember used to.

"Not having to eat Bernie's food!" Flarry replied.

Customers chuckled, including Bernie, who lounged at a table near the front of the store. "What's that?" he shouted, holding a hand to his ear. "Sorry. I couldn't hear you through my retirement."

Everyone burst out laughing again.

Meanwhile, over in the corner of the store, Clod, also wearing an apron, climbed a ladder. But he was too busy trying to impress a young Fire teenager to even notice the cans he was supposed to be stacking were rolling along the floor.

"If you were a vegetable, you'd be a *cute*-cumber," he told the giggling teen. Then, with effort, he pulled several flowers out from his armpit. "My queen."

By the smoke-reading room, Cinder emerged, holding the hands of a young Fire couple glowing with passionate colors.

"Everybody, we have a new match!" she announced. "And they *stink* of love!"

"Yeah!" the man exclaimed as everyone clapped. "We *reek*!"

From her vantage point, Ember took everything in. The Fireplace was back to normal, bustling with activity. But . . . it would never *quite* be normal again, would it? Not the normal she'd grown up with or the normal she remembered. But perhaps the normal that was meant to be all along.

From the front table, Ember felt her àshfá's gaze on her. She looked at him and smiled. The pride in his eyes—if bittersweet—was all worth it.

"Hey, everyone!" Wade's voice echoed from the front door.

"Hey, Wade!" everyone greeted him back.

Ember turned to him, taking note of the suitcase he was holding. She had known he would be carrying it. She had helped him pack it. So why did this still feel hard?

Wade took her hand and nodded encouragingly. "It's time."

A while later, the Lumen and Ripple families stood on the dock beside a large passenger ship ready to depart. Ember and Wade faced their parents, knowing it was time to board, not truly ready to go.

"You know, I'm not really one for tearful goodbyes." Wade's lower lip quivered.

"Oh, you big liar!" Brook wrapped her son in a fierce hug, sobbing. "Drip, drip, drip . . ."

"Goes the baby boy!" Wade finished along with her. They both bawled.

Bernie leaned over and whispered to Ember. "You sure about this one?"

Ember nodded. "I'm sure." Then her expression grew serious.

"Dad, I'm sorry the internship is so far away. I mean, it's the best glass design company in the world, but who knows if it'll become a real job, and it might not end up being anything—"

"Shhh." Bernie put his hand on his daughter's shoulder. Its warmth was familiar, like a comforting blanket. "Go. Start your new life. Your mother and I will be here."

Ember looked at Wade, breathing in the crisp, salty sea air. Their new adventure awaited. There was only one thing left to do.

Hand in hand, they walked toward the loading ramp leading up to the boat.

But just before her foot touched it, Ember stopped. She put down the suitcase. And she turned to her àshfá.

She could tell by the look that crossed his face he was concerned.

But he didn't have to be. He had given her everything she had ever needed and more.

Holding her hands before her, Ember bowed low in the ceremonial gesture of respect and love her àshfá had been denied years earlier.

When she looked up, Bernie's eyes glittered with tears of gratitude. He, too, bent low, returning the sacred bow.

Finally, Ember took hold of Wade's hand. The coolness of his hand bubbled against her palm. She would never take that hand or their shared chemistry for granted ever again.

"Are you ready?" Wade's eyes sparkled.

"I am." Ember's light shone.

And together, they stepped on the boat.